In the Foreboding Shadows of Holiness

Scott Shaw

Buddha Rose Publications

First Edition 1988
Second Edition 2010
Third Edition 2018

ISBN: 1-877792-17-9
ISBN-13: 9781877792175

Library of Congress: 2010941737

10 9 8 7 6 5 4 3 2 1

Printed in the United States of America

In the Foreboding Shadows of Holiness

Table of Contents

Introduction

War: there is always a war somewhere. War is where you make it.

For some people war seems to find them. Military war, physical war, psychological war, psychic war—war all the same.

This world, it is in flux. Nothing is stagnate. Nothing is forever. Movement from one to the other, from this on to that, from new onto the next, from youth to aged, unknown to known, innocent to tainted, from yours to mine. This is the basis for war.

I hate war. I hate conflict. Yet, in all its forms, all its destinies, I am the one which war seems to find.

I am a warrior; though I never chose it to be that way.

Choice forgotten—destiny takes hold...

Part I

It was Burma, I was there, as I had been before; *Burma Ma.*

I was in Burma, doing what I do as I travel; observe.

The observations were good. The lifestyle took hold of me. I did not feel separated or distant. I felt alive in the wisdom that the Goddess had bestowed upon me.

The weather, it was warm, as the climate of Southeast Asia promises. It was warm, but the winter, such as the Burmese winter is, it was coming upon us. Us, the Burman people, the foreign diplomats, the retired foreign officials, the expatriates, the travelers, the tourists, the academics, and I.

Me, I had arrived the night before; arrive in Mandalay. Arrived on a planned brief stay, in a minor city, in a diminutive country that only offered visas for a maximum stay of seven days.

I flew in. I was picked up at the airport. I arrived at the Mandalay Hotel; my usual haunt while in the city. Reservation upon arrival, null-and-void; none, *nada.* I was pissed, though I played it cool. I was pissed because I did not wish to spend my time in this city sleeping in one of the lice infested guesthouses that are frequented and inhabited by the international hippies. Lice infested with outhouses—no private baths. Me, I had come to prefer the ability to dine at a restaurant, located in the/this hotel; have a cold one upstairs in the upstairs bar. But, reservations, they had not heard my name. Did not have it upon their list.

I was about to become hostile, though I doubted it would have done any good. I was about to… But, then this small petite and beautiful lady emerged from a door and came to place herself behind the reservations desk. A lady I had never seen there before.

I had been the first. The first to make my way to the front. Knowing Southeast Asia; knowing life, I never let myself come in last. I had been the first off of the government, *"Tourist Burma,"* pickup truck that had been sent to meet the plane— the plane that I was on; to pick us up at the airport and to take us, (those upon the said plane), to our desired hotels and/or guesthouses.

The pickup truck: blue and small. Toyota, I think. We rode in the back; the luggage and the people. There are no taxis. No, not in Mandalay. No, not like Rangoon, where all the drivers want to buy your polo shirts, your levis, your sunglasses, your alcohol, your anything sellable…

But here, here in Mandalay, here in the North, the government holds a tighter rein on its people. They, the government, and the government officials, do not want people to stray too far, too much off the beaten path, too far from what is known/what is allow. No, not too far off into the restricted areas. No, not here, where they, the restricted areas, are at hand.

So, no. There are no taxis. At least none in the traditional sense of the word and/or ideology.

As such and because of, the government sends its blue and small pickup truck to take you, (me), from the airport to the hotel and/or the guesthouse of your choice.

Me, I was the first to approach the desk. I looked at the woman. You know, the woman I just described. She looked at me. We both studied the confusion—the confusion of those who, like I, had made reservations but did not have a reservation. Those like me, but not like me. No, they were not like me. No, not at all.

I was the first and the first to meet her eyes. I was young, single, unencumbered, long blond hair falling onto my shoulders. The others around me: married, together; none were apart. None were separate and available. No, not like me.

Our eyes met. She stood behind the counter and looked at me. She looked at the guest registry. She said something to the young man, hotel employee who also stood behind the counter; encountering all the confusion—dealing with it but not knowing what to do with it.

Her conversation completed. She looked up at me,

"Do you want a room?"
"Yes."
"Are you alone?"
"Yes."
"I think we have one for you."

I was in…

*   *   *

I waved farewell to my newfound friends. A German couple: a Ph.D. and a Ph.D. (I had not received my Ph.D. yet). He was called doctor and she was pissed because everyone called her misses. They were teaching in Chiang Mai, Thailand for a year. They had come to Burma for a little holiday. Holiday, on a maximum seven-day visa.

We had ridden the airplane north together— north from Rangoon. With my room key in hand, I smiled at them. I waved at them. I was gone.

I headed into the courtyard, down the corridor, my room to the left. AOK.

Inside, I found the typically humble accommodations of the Mandalay Hotel. Southeast Asian humble. But, neat and relatively clean. Relatively, in terms of Southeast Asia.

My bedspread, pink. My walls, green print. A drape covering my closet. The bathroom: a toilet, a sink, a shower curtain, a shower, which drained into the cement floor. AOK.

I relaxed for a moment/for a time. I lay on my bed.

It was afternoon when my plane had arrived. It was afternoon when I had checked into the hotel. Now, it was late afternoon. After a moment or three of reflection, I went out, out into the late afternoon/early evening air.

I went out with the fantasized intention of seeing my sweet, new found, Burmese receptionist impatiently awaiting my return at the desk of confusion.

I exit from my room. I walked by the desk cool and slow; glancing as I strutted my bad stuff by. I wanted her to be there, needed her to be there; knew she would be there. She was not.

I gave he, the young and otherwise overwhelmed male desk clerk, a casual nod as he looked up at my passing silhouette. He smiled. He had a nice smile. Seemed like a good dude. I immediately liked him.

It was out to the streets; turn left, as the feeling dictated. I walked, the streets of Mandalay. I looked at the moat around the palace and breathed in the air of the gardens of Mandalay.

The Streets of Mandalay, unlike *The Streets of San Francisco,* are were seasoned with the texture of the ages. South Asian goddess reigned in the realms of the ethereal and haunt this land with a promise of a passion that has never come to pass. The people dark. The culture old. Veering nowhere near the twentieth century.

Paved; some of Mandalay's streets are paved. Most are not—dirt roads. Some of the paving also produces sidewalks—such as sidewalks are in Mandalay. Most, do not.

The house(s)—homes to the people and the business; most, if not all, are made out of wood. Wood with some straw thrown in for good measure.

A few buildings; like the palace, like my hotel; made out a-concrete or components thereof. A few; but a very few.

The people, they walk. They pedal on their bicycles. A few trucks carrying cargo. Very few. A land lost in time/kept from time.

I think no words can ever truly describe this city. Can words ever truly describe any city? As such/and because of, I won't go into long boring verbal detail here about what the city looks like. Looks like here in the early to mid 1980s. There's a million books out there with photographs of this city. Yes, I am sure of that. I am sure, because I too have taken many of photograph of this geographic place in time. And, some—some have been published.

Look there, if you want to know. *For a picture paints a thousand words.*

*   *   *

I walked towards the city central—city central such as Mandalay has. I walked. I was greeted by the glances of the Burmans. Their dark skin caresses the deepening blue of the coming evening sky.

Clouds, I remember the clouds as I walked that day. White, large merging with the tops of the trees as I looked upward. Upward, as I walked onward—moving into destiny.

As I once again turned left, passing the soccer stadium, I was approached by a lady. She was large. Food had been good to her. She must have had plenty to eat.

"How are you, sir?"
"Good. And you?"
"Very good."
"Is this your first time to Mandalay?"
"No, I have been here before."
"Do you like antiques?"
"Only if they have a meaning."
"What do you mean, sir?"
"What do you mean?"

Though her English diction was adequate. She didn't quite get the gist of my inference. She thought for a moment, then she continued…

"I have a shop here. Perhaps you would like to come and look inside."
"Well… I don't think so. I'm just walking for now."

14

"That's fine, but please come back. My shop is right there."

She pointed to an old house with a sign that I may never have seen had I not been notified of its presence.

"Where did you learn to speak such good English," I asked.
"From the missionaries."

Oh, the missionaries…

My mind laughed as we parted, as I walked on; walked away. Missionaries…

*   *   *

Now, to give you the backstory; my main L.A. babe, (girlfriend of the time/at the time), and I had seen a movie two months ago—I guess it must have been two months before—before that, before this; before I had returned to Southeast Asia. We had seen it in Westwood; her and I. It was a movie of fighting. A movie of war. War, which this book is about. It was a movie with soldiers; soldiers in a foreign land. No, not an army, but a military; hired, and paid to kill. Mercenaries, they are commonly called.

We had left the theater after the movie. We were having a bite to eat, speaking of the movie. She said, *"Missionaries,"* when she meant *"Mercenaries."* She said to me in reference to the above. Missionaries, meaning mercenaries. We laughed as she caught her own verbal mistake.

Me, I laughed then, to myself, as I walked away. I laugh now. Laughed at the joke we had continued for the remaining time we had together in L.A. The remaining time before I had left, returned to my Southeast Asian wasteland, in search of the perfect Asian dream.

A joke, missionaries/mercenaries...

As she let me off at the airport; LAX, her parting words to me,

"Look out for the missionaries!"

*   *   *

Night was closing in. I looked around as I walked through one of Mandalay's outdoor food markets. The vegetables lay on the ground. Dirt was the name of the game here. The people crowded their way through. The people, dark. I was light.

They crowded their way through, making preparations for their evening meal. The market was full—full of the masses; dark, like the sky was becoming dark. Together; families in tow, families to feed.

I was alone. Light in this dark land. Dark that was merging into the night. Dark, like the color of night. Beautiful in its complexity. Beautiful in its illusion. The dark hides the light; hides the obvious. I embrace the dark.

The people who surrounded me were not particularly aware of my presence. No notoriety was gained. I was unique, in the masses/in these masses, yet I went unnoticed/unobserved. The Burmans, they had other things on their minds.

As I left the marketplace, the sky was fading to a deep blue. Seductive, like the veil of a hidden goddess.

May the goddess embrace me...

I returned to my hotel as fading light had reached its summit. It was dark.

Me, I switched back into my cool mode as I went by the desk; just in case the babe was in attendance. But, my longed for awaiting receptionist was not waiting—she was nowhere to be seen. I, however, did get a wave and a smile from the alright young dude, still manning the helm.

I did the brief wash up in my room and headed on towards my dinner. I was happy to see my Dr./Dr. friends had also gotten a room, *"A closet in the back,"* as they described it. But, it was a room. It was not a space/place in one of those horrible hippie guesthouses.

Dinner: onion soup, steak, mashed potatoes, and java, (real American). It went down good.

For lack of anything better to do. And, I mean come on... Not even a T.V. in my vacant hotel room. Well, in fact and in truth there are few T.V.s in Mandalay. That being stated, my room did not have much illusion to offer me. So me, I went out; outside/out there. I cooled my way past the desk, (still no-go in the babe department), and on out to the streets I went.

The night, it was a deep, dark. I walked the side streets of Mandalay. I felt alert, aware, and yet safe like I was in the arms of a known lover. I was alone, except for the noise that came from the wooden houses, and the occasional passing bicyclist who would say, *"Hello." "Peace."* They all say, *"Peace,"* in Burma. Where did they learn it? I do not know. But, what I do know, is that this/this writing is about war... So, let's forget the subject of peace, at least for right now.

I walked on. The bugs flew rampant wherever there was light. But, me, I continued deeper-and-deeper into the Mandalay night; trying to keep track of the blocks I had passed; trying to remember the corner(s) I had turned—trying, for I knew, were I to become lost in this dark, in this night, I may never-ever find my way back/may never find my way home.

In actuality it was like a flashback from the last time I took acid back in old Hollywood. Yeah, I had just started Hollywood High School. What was I? I must have been fifteen. Yes, fifteen. For it was Halloween night, October 31st. This guy and I—a schoolmate, we had met midway/mid range; *en route* to a party. A high school party. We meet in the middle, for he traveled from his lavish home in the Hollywood Hills. Me, I walked from the gutters on the wrong side of the tracks. But, me and him/him and I, we *duped* up. We took way too much *A* in a telephone booth on Beachwood and Franklin. *Orange Sunshine* and *Blotter.* Then, we cruised onto the party, a mile or so away—over and off of/between Santa Monica Blvd. and Melrose. We walked. But, nothing, *nada.* I was not coming on. He was not coming on. Time passed... Then, as we sat against a wall inside the apartment, listening to *Led Zeppelin* blast from the speakers, it hit—it hit us both. Hit us, like full-on over the head. The trails, they etched everything in red. Every word, every sound, turned into an echo. I tried to lie down. I could not. He pulled me up; suggesting that we try to walk it off a bit, get some air.

Outside, we rounded the block. I was lost into the realms of the abstract. He was mumbling incoherently. I tried to remember the way back, back to the apartment. The apartment, my only source of physical reference. I counted the number of corners as we turned them. Knowing four. Yes, there must be four. This was a city block; right? Four corners. It must have four corners!

But, somewhere in all the illusion, I lost count. I remember, coming upon the sounds, coming upon the people, coming upon the police; who had arrived at the scene. I did not know where I was.

Burma, I counted. I remembered. I walked, deeper, yet I felt secure. Not lost and afraid like that night in Hollywood. I felt secure as the fool feels secure. Secure in his ignorance. I felt safe. No danger. I was a fool.

*   *   *

Danger comes in many forms; in many shapes, in many sizes. I walked on. I was walking into a trap. A trap I never saw coming.

I returned to the hotel that evening; waltzed past the desk, no babe. All I had, all I was left with, is the memory of that walk. That walk, which I detail for you here.

With only the memory of the walk to chalk up for the experience, I knew/assumed that there had to be something more. Something more to remove the label of, *"Nothing special,"* from this evening. This evening, my first one back in Mandalay.

It was early—early by my standards, early by Bangkok standards. Bangkok, where I had just spent the past few weeks. Early, maybe seven thirty, eight, or so. Mandalay rolls the rug up early. Still in no mood to return to my room, I went upstairs to the bar area. You know, the hotel bar I previously mentioned. The one that is upstairs. Upstairs, in like a mezzanine area. Upstairs, thought the Mandalay Hotel has only one floor. One floor, but it does have its bar on its mezzanine.

I get up there. I order up a large one. A large bottle of Mandalay Beer.

"You have been here before."

So said the barkeep.

"Yes, you remember me?"
"No, I remember the glasses. But your hair, your hair is longer now."
"Yes, it is."

My hair, my long blond hair. The last time I was in Burma, it had been a bit shorter—growing out. Me, coming out of the L.A. punk rock scene. Coming out of a motorcycle accident that almost killed me where they had shaved my waist length dreadlocks to cut into my head; remove the bones of my face, from my brain. Heal me/save me. Did they succeed? I don't know?

My glasses… My now traditional tortoise shell brown and dark and round sunglasses. Yes, I was sprouting them, even at night.

Usually in the night, I wore my habitual, *"Old man glasses,"* as I call 'em. Dark colored plastic on the top, steel on the bottom. You know, straight out of the 1940s. Yeah, in the night, they were the ones that were commonly in place, (or none at all). But, here/tonight, I preferred to hide. Hide, deep within the realms of distant eyes.

You know the eyes are the keys to the soul. So me, I wore my sunglasses.

There was conversation, predominantly in German rattling through the lounge. A lot of Germans seem to hit Southeast Asia. There was noise. A lot of noise. The voices blended into one another. And, the fan up above, latched into the ceiling, it went round-and-round-and-round.

I saw an empty table. I pulled up a chair. It was wooden. The table and the chair. The table, wooden brown. The chair, its wooden arms and legs were painted green.

Me, I settled in. Put the bottle on the table. The glass in my hand. I knew it/could feel it, there was no better place to be in this world. No, not this night.

I had killed one of the bad pups, very large bottles; went up to the bar and had gotten another. I chilled back, in my chair and was letting the evening roll on.

Into the scene rolls this bad little Asian dude with two high dressed/high fashion ladies in tow. The three of them, obviously Chinese by bloodline, hit a table and ordered up a round of the poison.

The group did not turn the eyes of most of the constituents in this establishment—tourists, the all of them. They, the tourists, did not stop their conversations, predominantly in German, discussing where they had been, what they seen—their lives, their home, their etcetera, and their so on's... The people did not hush their noise level; most did not even bat an eye. Bat an eye and observe that we were in Burma, and in walks this three of a kind.

The man looked to be mid-forties, dressed in a relatively nicely tailored dark blue suit—relative in terms of this being Burma. The two women, early thirties, clad in evening gowns. One white. And, the other, the one that caught my eye, pink.

I thought to myself, *"Am I being too judgmental? But, I mean come on... This is Burma. No, not Thailand. No, not the Philippines. No, not Singapore. Men do not dress in dark blue suits and ladies simply do not wear this Southeast Asian high fashion."*

Now there are many of the Chinese bloodline living within Burma's bounds. And, this crew was obviously local. But, this is Mandalay. A dark blue suit? Nobody wears suits in Mandalay! Hell, even me, who always wears either a suit or a sport coats; I had even left mine in my room this night.

And/Plus/Etcetera, this is Burma; evening gowns, even for the beautiful, they are not known.

The makeup that adorned the women's eyes was thick; jewelry, it was gaudy and obvious. They looked to me to be straight from a massage parlor in Bangkok.

But me, there I sat, all alone. Perhaps if I had been involved in one of the conversations that were taking place around me, my mind wound have not been sent into the realms of wonderment. But, *"If,"* is too big of a word for me.

The case was, I was not in one of those conversations. As such, my observations must have become evident, for as I sat there drinking from my glass, I apparently was none-too-casually staring. From this, the sweet young woman in the white, low-cut, evening gown, tipped her glass my direction. I, being the gentleman that I am, tipped mine back at her. *Back at you, babe.* From this, the course of destiny was set in motion...

She then leaned over to her two friends and whispered something. They all turned. They all smiled. They all lifted their glasses and gave me the *cheers.* Back your direction, dude and dudettes.

*   *   *

I continued on with my brew as I tried to not stare so overtly. Finishing the bottle, and in my progressively intoxicating state, *"What the hell,"* I thought, I decided to have one more round for the road, *the hard road.*

Me, I walked up to the bar; past the three highly dressed, previously mentioned individuals. I kept my eyes focused, straight-ahead, the bar in sight/insight. I did not look at them.

"One more Mandalay Beer, please."

The barkeep dished it out. I forked over the Burmese cash. A one hundred note.

As I was awaiting my change, I find the blue suit man standing to my side. My left side.

"Are you German?" He inquired
"No, American."
"Oh, I thought with the blond hair and all..."
"Sorry," I said.

My mind, due to the intoxicating effect of the ale was saying, *"Fuck you. I ain't no fucking German."* But I was cordial.

"Can I buy you a drink," he asked.
"Got my passion right here." I answered.
"Passion?"

He didn't really get what I meant. None-the-less, he asked,

"Would you like to come and sit with me and my friends?"
"My friends and I," I countered.

The look of confusion came to his eyes, as he obviously did not get the joke of my correcting his English grammar. So, I nonchalantly inquire,

"Oh, you have friends here?"

He didn't get that either. So again, I was forced to speak,

"Sure."

Motion takes on its own forms. Its own forms in its own perplexities. It is motion still the same. Movement to the source. A movement that I was happy to make.

*   *   *

The blue suit dude graciously pulled up another green chair with wooden arms and legs to his table. I thanked him and sat down. My bottle and my glass in hand. The lady dressed in white immediately reached for my bottle, reached for my glass, and began to pour a drink for me. Asia, a chauvinist's delight.

Introductions were made all around. There English was, well, passable... Their names; unimportant...

They talked in small talk. I dislike small talk.

"Are you a tourist?"
"No."
"Oh, are you here on business?"
"No."

They looked at each other.

"What do you do?"
"I'm a dreamer."
"A dreamer?"

They discuss the matter among themselves in a dialect of Chinese that I didn't really understand. They came to what appeared to be an appropriate translation. All smiles.

I sat there. The distance of the drink had already taken me over. I felt the space.

I suppose I should have been happy for I was meeting and talking with this group that had drawn my attention: the ladie(s) and the dude. Drawn my attention, but no one else's interest in the place. But, that is life; isn't it? We each project our own realms of reality. Project, like the projectionist in a theater of movies.

I suppose I should have been happy for cultural walls were falling down and observations were being made. Made of this strangely dressed crew. Strangely, for Mandalay. Strangely, for Burma. I suppose… But, I was surprisingly disinterested; distant—no doubt due to the drink.

Disinterest in their words. Disinterested in their attire. Disinterested in their ethnic origins.

Even, semi-disinterested in the ladies who occupied two of the chairs at the table where I sat.

Funny, a few brews in me and my attention is generally set on objects of the opposite sex. But, this time it/I was not.

In truth, it is hard for me to remember exactly, moment-to-moment, what took place as I sat at the table. We sat, and drinks were pounded down. Hard for me to remember, no doubt due to post my third bottle of Mandalay Beer, I hit another, and another, and another, and another.

Now, you have to put this session of the drink into context. Remember, these are the large Asian beer bottles that are not brewed with the societal morals and constraints of the western world. So, they have more alcohol in them. Plus, they are equivalent to about three brewskis each.

Disinterest and the poisonous ale, the root to all intoxicated forgetfulness.

What happened in words, to the best of my recollection, did not seem to matter much. But, in the fog/my fog, I was told the ladies were his sisters. Sisters of the dude. *"Yeah, right,"* I thought. He was a businessman. They were businesswomen. *"Business of the night,"* is what came to my mind.

The one in the white was like way digging my scene. It was obvious. Digging my scene or digging my grave, I never was quite sure which.

Though she was not so un-anything, her features were not so fine; not as fine as the lady wearing the hazy shade of pink, who looked on, all smiles, as her sister, *her sister of the night,* continued to pour my drinks.

The small talk of their family being in Burma for three generations seemed to matter less-and-less. The drink, the moment, the hand that eventually found its way upon my knee, lend me to have other things, other destinations, in mind.

I stood up. I kicked down the last full glass from my bottle of ale. I one-sipped it.

"So are we going to party?"
"Party?"

Came the question from the mouth of the blue suit dude.

"Party."

The three looked at each other and begin discussing the matter in Chinese.

"Would you like her to come to your room tonight?"

He, the blue suit, was referring to the lady dressed in white.

"No, I want her."

The Chinese kicked in again.

"It is better if you go with her."
"But I want her."
"In the dark, my American friend, what does it matter?"
"In the dark is the only place that it does matter, my Burmese friend."

I could see that he did not like my referring to him as Burmese. For all he talked of that evening was his Chinese heritage. But, fuck him. I knew exactly what I was doing when I chose those words.

For the record. For those of you who may not know. The Chinese in Burma, and for that matter, virtually all other geographical locations across the globe, are very proud of being Chinese and not of the indigenous stock. That said. That's why I chose my words as I did.

"Well, you make up your mind, I'm in room seventeen."

I walked away sleek and cool. As I always do, even when I am more than a bit tilted.

I went down the stairs from the bar and out, into/onto the un-fanned, mild winter heat of Mandalay that permeated the open-air accommodations of the Mandalay Hotel. The air felt good.

I walked past the desk, just in case... No luck on the Eastern front. The desk service was shut down.

I went to/into my room. I flicked on the light. I closed the door behind me. I checked my bed just to make sure there was no large bugs or lizards on it. Bugs or lizards as I have found there in the past.

The bed, it was clean. I flicked off the light. I flopped on the bed and said to myself, *"If that chick comes a knocking, fuck her, I just want to sleep."*

*   *   *

The moment of truth rolled around a bit faster than I had anticipated, however. A knock on the door. Pink? White? My mind questioned... A second knock. I got up. Opened the door. White it was.

She began to go into some discussion of apologies, of whys, hows, wherefores, and this time of the month... I said, *"Shuuuu."*

I pulled her in. Closed the door. Led her to my bed. Pushed her down. And that, my friends, was that.

*   *   *

She kissed good. I like women who know how to kiss. I especially love hookers that can kiss good.

Kissing... Something a whore will rarely do...

I guess she was from the out-back. Didn't know the rules...

Post the lip lock(s), she went right for my love rod and grabbed hold—gnawing and pulling at it through my pants. I realized that this was going to be a *no-holds-barred* session. I like 'em that way.

I reached into her gown, lowed its low-cutness, and exposed her small left breast. Her age showed just a bit in the slight sag that accompanied it. There were also a few stretch marks that were beginning to take hold. But, none-the-less, I had to go for a little love lickin' session, while pulling down the dress. As I outed the other one; the other boob.

I then went for the crotch. No underwear. Oh yes, I did like Asia. Soup was already on and she was pulling the ankle lengthness of her dress up to her waist, revealing her sparsely haired Chinese pussy. I unzipped and put the power pup home. Smooth, it went in so smooth.

We humped and thumped for a time. She was as breather/a screamer. I laid the slobs—dug the tongue in deep. I kissed her face, licked her face. I could taste the makeup in my mouth. I was smearing it just fine.

I rolled her over; let her take her turn at the helm. She power fucked me but it was uneventful. Soupy though. Yes, she was very soupy. I could feel it painting itself upon my skin.

Now, I was intoxicated, and intoxication, such as it is, leaves a dude with a bit of a problem of blowing the cookies. So, I let her chill and thrill up topside until she gave the basic motions of she had her orgasmic fill.

Can a hooker ever cum? Yes, they can.

So, I rolled the situation back over and choked and stroked it. It did take some time but the rocks did finally blow.

Did her, *Raw Dog*. No rubber.

Nothing so special. Nothing so new. Just the same old feeling of that not so sensual, not so traumatic, orgasm of intoxication.

I pulled out. I pulled off. I zipped up the drawers.

"You are very good, Mr. American friend."
"I know."

She giggled.

"You're dismissed."
"What?"
"You can go now."

"Don't you want me to stay? Won't you need me in the morning?"
"No, I will probably need a doctor in the morning."
"A doctor? Why?"

She didn't get the joke. Me, I figured I was going to have a kill hangover.

"What's the price?"
"How much you like it, Mr. American friend."

I pulled out five; five hundred, that is, in hundred-dollar Burmese notes.

I helped her pull her dress down—as it had been pulled up. I pushed her to the door.

I grabbed her. I turned her around. I gave her one last kiss for the remembrance; one last kiss goodbye. Then, I gave her a shove out the door and she was gone.

Me, I hit the bed. And, I was out. Out, like the lights. Out, like my five hundred Burmese *kyat*. Gone, to the realm of where only the goddess of the night holds the keys to the lock.

Part II

The next morning comes on, as the next morning(s) tend to do. The morning after, as it were. I awoke 10:00 A.M.ish and checked my body to see what condition my condition was in. I had truly expected like a mega uck hangover. But, I felt AOK.

The next test, out of bed, hit the shower. The cold cement floor of the bathroom burned my feet in its frigidness. Ah, where were the five-star hotels of Bangkok?

The shower went on good though. The water a bit yellow. But hey, this is Burma after all.

I felt amazingly good. A good, which I did not expect. It must have been the fact that I had spent the last several months in a virtual continuum of drunken stupors and the hangovers seem to get less-and-less, as the endurance got built up. But, too much beer always hits me hard. Vodka being my preferred poison. But, this was Burma and no vodka to be had. So... Maybe it was the brand of beer or maybe it was a clean brew. I don't know? Even some western brews... They're dirty. They get me sick if I even look at them too long. But, anyway, for whatever reason, I was full-on.

Dressed... Out the door I strut.

By the desk. And yes, there she was. The hotel clerk of my dreams—my current fantasy. Our glances met. Our smiles met. Love, it was in the making. I even got a smile from the friendly young desk-hand, confusion jockey.

What could I say to the sweet young lass but, *"Good morning."* I was on my way to a bit of a chow session at the hotel restaurant.

Post and after. With the basics completed. I was on my way out and onto the illusion. A cool pass by the desk, complete with rehearsed words and promises in mind... But, my object of affection was not at hand. So, to the streets I went.

I decided that this day, my course would be Mandalay Hill. Mandalay Hill, towering far above the farmlands and the city below. I cut to the right, then to the left, around the Royal Palace grounds, complete with its moat. The walk and the sun it went on good.

I do not know exactly how far it is from the hotel, maybe a mile or three. I had a few offers from the bicycle taxi guys, but my feet generally prefer the travel, and dreams that lie young and awaiting.

I hit the surrounding areas; checked out a few of the local haunts; such as they are. You know, made out of wood and straw, of course.

I looked into the graveyard. And, had a local cola.

*   *   *

It was hot as I headed to the base of the holy hill.

Once at the base, I looked up at the thousands of concrete steps. They await in front of me to make my progression/my ascent towards the top. A thousand steps to reach the pinnacle of holiness for Burma.

For the uninitiated, Mandalay Hill is a large mountain which rest central to the city. It is home of many Buddhas and many steps to reach said Buddhas. Said steps to reach the top/reach the apex where one may view the vastness of *Mata Burma.*

The vastness and the Buddhas *en route.* Vastness and the Buddha, the pathway of the holy.

*   *   *

I hit the first step, the second step, and had sat down at the third, not wanting to get my feet too dirty from the dirt on the ground before my initial assent. I had sat down and just then, this little local chick decided it was her job to instruct me that I was being dis-reverent by placing my shoes anywhere upon the all-so-holy cement stairs of this sacred hill.

Now, Burma is in a country where they have neon lights, vibrating disco style, around the head of a statue of the Sakyamuni Buddha. Disrespectful? But, anyway…

Her mother told her to chill. Me, I almost felt bad for I like to respect the customs of a country. But, I was already sitting down and my shoes were already coming off by the time she spoke. So, so much for the scolding.

My shoes… I remember them well. They were *Puma Power Cats;* running shoes. Now, I always travel in a pair of the bad boy running shoes. They are great for the ten, twenty miles of waking I generally do per day.

I remember them well. It was the last journey that I set out upon with them in tow. They, the company, has stopped making them. I have had to switch to other brands/other names. But, I remember them… Yes, I remember. I remember those days; one of those feelings that you wish you could live again.

But, and in any case, with my shoes off, I decided they would be best placed in my camera backpack. So, I pulled out two of my 35mm cameras; two of the three. Replaced the space with shoes. The shoes were, in fact, an enormous amount lighter than said cameras.

I threw the cameras over my shoulder and up the hill, Mandalay Hill, I went.

Now, there can be no denying that it is a steep hall up that bad dude; stair-after-stair-after-stair. I do not know how many. I do not know how far. I'm sure that it is stated, for the record, in some travel book. But, whatever it is, it is a-ways.

Me, I had to have me a periodic local cola or thirty *en route* up.

It was hot. It was steep, like the love sizzling off the morning cool in an Asian temple of tantric love.

I had gone maybe three quarters of the way when I hear,

"Pretty." A female voice was speaking my direction.
"No, handsome." Corrected by another female voice.

I had come upon this group of young souls, transversing the mountain. A group of five, six, or seven. The numbers they actually escape me. Boys and girls, men and women, ages, nineteen, twenty, twenty-one maybe.

It was all smiles and little talk. At least in terms of their understanding of the English language.

What could I do? I walked on, with just a passing smile. Like, what could I say to such a compliment? A compliment that I knew to be true.

Walk on/walk up. I took some photographs of various golden Buddhas, various shrines, various landscape scenes upon the way, and drank some more local cola.

Funny, I virtually never drink colas and soft drinks Stateside. But, out here in the outback; out on the hard road, you can't drink the water. That is you can't drink the water if you don't want to get sick. And, you have to drink something... So, a few upward bound local colas, purchased from the strategically located, local cola vendors. Up, I walked up...

I knew my body would be sore the day next. But, what could I do?

Other than that, I was, however, quite surprised at my seeming agility at having come out of my corner, full-on, post a night doused in the toxic liquid and bouncing, up-and-down, feverishly upon a babe that I never caught her name. Well, at least I don't remember it if she did tell it to me.

I walked on... Knowing the top was farther but wondering why it had to be so.

Finally, atop the top, our paths crossed again. That is the path of the young admiring group of passerby's and myself. You know, the group of five, six, or seven, I just mentioned.

I, in fact, did not know how this came to be; for I had not seen them go by. They must have passed me while I was taken a photograph or changing one of my lenses. Or, maybe it was when I was at a local cola shop. I do not know. But, and in any case, smiles were again exchanged.

Nothing lost, nothing gained... Again, they went their way, I went mine.

*   *   *

The summit; below stretched the green fields of the cultivated Burmese landscape. The sky was crystal blue. A cloud or two haunted its vastness. The temperature was warm—warm, not hot. Yet, the assent up the stairs, by the Buddha(s), by the shrine(s), was not exceedingly pleasant.

At the top, I sat to one side. The East side, I believe. The side just below the actual Buddha shine/chiseled Buddha summit. Just below, where one must climb a bit more concrete to pay final homage to that oh-so-sacred incarnation. The image of Siddharta Gutama, the Sakyamuni Buddha; formed and surrounded by cement.

I sat, having a cold one. A local cold one. A cold cola that is. *Give it to me straight, straight out of the bottle.*

I was more than cautious, as the vendors like to pour the bottled drinks in a dirty glass over local ice. They try to do this all the time. But, the local ice being formed out of local water, and you know all the stories about that…

I also had to be careful about drinking from one of those previously used straws, which all the locals always seem to desire. Used by many, how many others? Who knows? But, after being used, they are strategically placed, by the local cola vendors, in a neatly arranged local vase like object. Neatly placed, but never washed. So, I'm sure you catch my meaning about why I do not drink out of said receptacles.

Me, with drink in hand, I stared out onto the horizon. Burma, *Burma Ma.* Vast, old, touched, but renewing constantly.

"May I ask you a question?"

The words are spoken from the mouth of this traditionally dressed, based in tones of red and brown, young and more than beautiful Burmese girl.

"Sure, of course."
"Are you from Germany?"
"No, America."
"Oh, I have heard that your country is very beautiful."
"Yes, it is."

Her dark skin moved with her dark eyes and her innocence melted my soul.

"Is this your first time to Mandalay Hill?"
"No, I have been here before."
"Did you know that the Japanese in World War II took over Mandalay Hill?"
"Yes."
"Did you know they used it for a lookout post?"
"Yes."
"Did you know that they destroyed many shrines on it?"
"Yes. That is war."

She continued,

"Do you like Burma?"
"Yes, I love Burma. Especially the North. Like here in Mandalay."
"What do you do in America?"
"Nothing. What do you do in Burma?"
"I go to school."

"Then why are you up here?"
"I help my family sell drinks at that stand. The one you purchased the drink you are drinking from."

People passed as we spoke. They were residence on a religious retreat. They study me: my long blond hair, my numerous earrings, my very expensive cameras. They study me, but their images have only peripheral effect on my field of vision, as I am hypnotized by this young goddess's presence.

"Where did you learn to speak such perfect English?" I ask.
"From the missionaries."

Missionaries, I again laugh to myself.

"Do you know how old I am," she asks with a twinkle in her eyes.
"No."
"Guess."

Now, I play the compliment game. You know, the compliments that stroke the mind of a child.

"Seventeen."
"No, I am thirteen."
"Oh, you look so mature."
"Do you really think so?"
"Yes, of course."
"How old are you?"
"I'm an old man, twenty-seven."
"No, you're not old at all. You're the perfect age for a man."

She hesitates, then continues,

"Are you married?"

I smile,

"No."
"Would you like to be?
"Sure. When I meet the right girl."
"Maybe I'm the right girl. Would you like to marry me?"

What could I say to that?

"I would like to go to your country," she continues.
"I wouldn't."

There is a seriousness about her. About her voice, about her words, about the intensity of her eyes. Her seriousness is mesmerizing.

"You are very beautiful. May I take a picture of you?"
"Yes."

Uncool me... I ran out of film in my camera with the preferred focal length lens. I had to put a new roll in.
I felt uncomfortable, unprepared, untimely. My type A-personality and my self-consciousness kicked in. She was cool about it though. She studied my movements. Witnessed my course of action, as the film was properly placed.

"Okay."

The picture taken. I have it in mind and in physical form to this day. Her soul locked to mine, forever-and-ever-and-ever.

Our conversation goes on. We speak of Burma. We speak of the winter coming on. And, we speak of America.

Her perfection. Her deeply rooted wisdom— *the wisdom of a child.* It/she astonished me.

I conclude that she was/is the perfect being, in the perfect space, in the perfect place in my life. Though she implied it first, I ask her to marry me. She says that she will. She tells me that she must wait until she's fifteen, however—by law/by custom. I ask her to promise to wait for me. She tells me that she will.

Now, you gotta understand here, this is no weird pedophilia *thAng* on my part. In fact, and in truth, I virtually never verge more than a year or two my junior whenever, and if ever, I hook up with a younger woman. But this; her and I, it was all something much more profound/much more metaphysical. She had seen what she wanted/what she needed/embraced her destiny, and she came to me. Me, one who waltzes/dances in the world of mystical knowledge, I understood that this was a true meeting of our souls. So, I gave her the only thing that I could; a projected promise of tomorrow. If only I could live that long and make it back to her.

That was then. Now, by time/by spirit, she must be fifteen; perhaps sixteen. This, the tale you are reading, all took place two and a half/three years ago. Two and a half/three years ago, as these pages are being penned.

Me, sadly I have not returned to Burma since. But the memory of her, it is so clear.

I think it is truly my loss. My loss; not spending the rest of my days/my life with her.

She was whole. She was perfect. She possessed deep-deep knowledge. My loss; but probably not hers. As there are so many better men than I in this world. Those with job; real jobs. Careers. No mind for the metaphysics. No mind for the dreams. Just a mind for reality—for what is right in front of them.

Me, what was right in front of me was this dream of a perfect metaphysical child, who had found what she was looking for—me. All I had to do was wait. Wait and then come back in a couple of years. Yeah, there she was, right in front of me. A child and a concrete Buddha. All the elements for making the perfect life concoction. The perfect poem. The ultimate poison.

Do her thoughts ever go to me? Is she still waiting? Has another promising American, who arrived at the right place, at the right time, when she was fifteen years of age, taken her? I do not know.

And, if I had the money. If I had the means. I would fly back to her, right now.

But, then/not here/not as I write these pages, we parted company. I have a photo of her. It is slightly out of focus. It reminds me of her form, her perfection, her desire for me, and the life I could have/should have lived…

*   *   *

I proceeded downward.

Downward, following the same path that I had taken going up. The heat, the sweat(ing), the alcohol remaining in my body, and the lack of proper liquid content thereof and there for. I stopped for another round of the soda pop at a soda pop stand.

I was alone at the stand. Alone with another Burmese young lady. She was dressed in a white-based floral type traditional outfit. Traditional, in the sense that they all seem to wear wrap-around skirts and western style tops.

"Are you German?"
"No, American."

I am more than tired of forever, internationally, answering that question...

"Can you guess how old I am?"

Similar questions. I wondered, *"Do they rehearse these questions in soda pop school?"*

I guess, I played the game. She too was thirteen. *Soda pop school education?* Not near as beautiful as the previous teenager. A bit more round, if you know what I mean. But, I was on a roll and the promises of marriage and waiting for me were made.

Perhaps in all my foolishness and American ego, it is there that I somehow prostituted my sweet and first young love proposal in Burma by making it such a light subject with the secondary young love. Maybe, I do not know?

Maybe because of it/because of my words/my actions, I lost my chance of eternal first Burma love?

*   *   *

I will dispense with the formalities, the words spoken, the lies told—after a few, I was out-a-there and in the decent motion.

As I proceed in my downward strut. Down, in general, being a lot easier than up. At least where the stairs of Mandalay Hill are concerned; there on a bench, on a cement bench, to the side was a gathering of my fine young complimentary friends. You know the ones...

"You are very handsome," I once again hear.

From there, the conversation went on. Now I say, *"On,"* for they did speak English, just not very well. No, not at all.

I guess they had not been schooled by the missionaries, as had my first young case of Burmese love.

*   *   *

To describe this group. To give you a better understanding and a little bit better mental photograph; the group consisted of three women: one very Burmese dark, wearing bright red lipstick. Another girl was Burmese, lighter skinned, with more of a fashionable hairdo.

Perhaps at this point, I can interject a brief observation. Burma, for all its removed-ness, many of the ladies, and some of the dudes, had very *bitch'n* hairdos. I mean, now, we are talking deep Southeast Asia here, on the periphery of South Asia. Yet, it is easy to see guys with long, styled hair, and women sprouting modern western *'dos.'*

This is very different, on the whole, from say even, Thailand, which is much more wealthy and western inclined than Burma. But, I mean, like in Rangoon, the capitol of Burma, you even find European rock music magazines.

Anyway, with that knowledge at hand, back to the story…

And, a third girl; a lady indeed. The one who had corrected the red lip-sticked girl of her improprieties from, *"Pretty,"* to, *"Handsome."* She was light golden skinned—had black, fashionably cut, hair. Carried an umbrella in her hand to protect her fair skin from the sun. And yes, though we were in Burma, she was oh so Chinese. And, on so fine… A fucking goddess, if I ever saw one.

Damn, right place, right time, I guess. Two straight-up goddesses in such a short etching of time and space. The one, thirteen. And, this one, a bit older; of legal age.

The dudes in tow/in the group seemed far less important. At least in my mind. Though they were, I suppose, indeed nice enough. Dark skinned Burmans, the both of them. Short black hair. One wore a tee-shirt; the other wore a blue button-up.

We spoke, exchanged comments, and proceeded the rest of the way down Mandalay Hill together. Upon reaching the bottom, they easily slipped on their sandals. Me, I had to deal with the realities of life, as such, and pull my socks and shoes out of my backpack, replace my cameras, and put my bad *Puma Power Cats* back on and in place. They, the crew, more-or-less patiently waited.

We headed over to a local cola stand and ordered up a round. Some of them had this local concoction out of a jar, which I could see had things floating in; i.e. dirt and the etcetera. Me, I went for another of the bottled local colas. Though a bit more pricey, a lot more safe. So, I thought... That is until the soda gent so kindly poured it over local ice, in a local used and dirty glass, complete with a local and previously used straw, before I could say, *"No."*

I mean, come on, I was distracted with this/that sweet young lady. You know the one, Chinese via Burma. The one with the umbrella to protect her from the sun.

"Sick," I thought. *"This is it. I am going to get sick!"*

I, at least, pulled the straw out. But, the heat and sun melted the ice very quickly.

I tried to *play it cool* and not power the soda down to precede the melt. But, in the *playing it cool,* I couldn't shoot it. I had to sip it. Thus, and because of, the said local ice did its melting.

We all drank our poisons and *rap'd* as it were. They were college students. Finishing up their finals at the local institution of higher education. They were due for winter recess, and/or winter graduation. They were all non-locals having slid into Mandalay from all over Burma.

The *convo* was good. Enlightening in its own way.

They, the students, were all, fully way interested in me. Which was all fine and good with me, as I hoped it would be a passageway in the direction of the starry-eyed lady of a Chinese/Burmese college student, who held an an umbrella in her hand.

Local colas absorbed, they had to head on back for further finals. Me, I was chilling down and gettin' ready for my traditional afternoon nap. We parted company. Plans were made, I was invited by the obvious commandant of the crew, the blue button-up shirt dude, to meet for dinner. Invited by their invitation. Tonight—that night.

I headed forward on foot, turning down a bike ride on their handlebars. They unchained and mounted their bikes. Those bad little Southeast Asian kind of bicycles—similar in texture and design to the old Schwinn's of the 1950's. I further turned down a ride on one of the three-wheel bicycle taxis that inhabit the city of Mandalay. The dude thinking, I did not understand him, attempted translation through the students. I laughed. I did understand. Me, I still declined.

I walked... As I walked, the group passed me by me in full-on, full force. Like a bunch of mislead/misdirected bikers riding their hogs, flying their colors, and screaming to the banshees of the night.

But, this was not the night. This was the daylight. And, there she was, this goddess of a lady. And, I do not use that word lightly. A lady, and in Burma. It/she did take my breath away.

She, the Chinese sub-princess, riding sidesaddle on the back of one of the bad dudes bikes. Her blue silk sarong skirt blending into the forms of the day. Her white shirt accenting her pale golden skin, with a blue umbrella held over her head. The sun, much too hot for someone as delicate as she.

Me, I was out of my socks in serious love with her. Love such as it were.

As I walked, the bicycle taxi driver again came up to me and asked again if I wanted a ride. I, in truth, told him that I did not have any money. I mean, I did have some when I set out that morning. It was some left-over change from the five hundred *kyat* I threw down; absorbed into the pussy of that nighttime goddess, of evening last. But, after breakfast and all the local colas and stuff, I was chill factor zero in the money department.

He insisted that was no problem and that he was going in the direction of my hotel anyway. And, he really wanted to give me a ride. What could I say?

I climbed up into the bad back seat of his three-wheeled trike. And, we were off.

The driver surprisingly spoke pretty good basic English. Learned from the tourists, he explained. Not the missionaries.

His English was, in fact, better than the students that I had met. He asked me if they were my friends. I explained they were students and I had just met them. He told me that by his speaking with them, (you know when he asked them to translate), he knew they were not originally from the Mandalay area. Dialectic accents, I guess. He especially couldn't understand, *"The Chinese girl,"* as he called her. The one I had my eye on. I laughed to myself. But, I will explain the whole Chinese Burma *thAng* in a moment.

As we drove through the mild heat and the landscape of Mandalay, we continued our conversation. He explained that before he drove the bicycle taxis, he was a monk. I told him I too was once a monk. He told me, now, he was married and had a child. I told him I was not married and did not have a child. As we continued our ride, he said he wanted to teach me Burmese. Why not? He taught me, *"How are you?"* *"Nay gaun tee lah?"* I told him, *"Thank you."* He said, *"Amya e jay zu tin ba day."*

We came upon my hotel. I scraped my pockets and gave him the few Burmese currency notes I had left. Two or three, I think. I apologized, he didn't mind. I did.

He was such a nice guy; late thirties, dressed in red raggy pants, a brown raggy skirt, and the years of age wore into his skin; making it look raggy—similar, at least in arrangement, to the clothes upon his back. I never saw him again.

No money in tow, I passed the desk. There she was my Burma queen. I smiled. She smiled. I walked to my room. Inside, I pulled out, from the hidden compartment in my suitcase, traveler's checks. Three hundred, U.S. I looked at my Rolex, it was two o'clock exactly. I walked back in the direction of the desk, to get my currency exchanged.

"Hello, Mr. Slam."
"Please call me Samuel."
"Do you want to exchange some money?"
"Yes, please."

Exchange, I did. A move I made. There is little time on a maximum seven-day visa to play any games…

Nanda Soe was her handle. She was small; maybe five foot nothing. Thin; her dark skin was outlined in perfection by her black hair, high cheekbones, and almost round eyes.

Interest was obvious: no doubt on her part; no doubt on mine.

But, my paranoid American mind saw a green card in one of her eyes, a dollar sign in the other. But, if you want to play, you've got to pay.

Cool? Cool. Yes, I was cool. I checked it out to see what time she was off—not trying to push too hard, too fast. But, I had to push, just fast enough. There was time; she worked into the evening hours of five o'clock.

Currency was exchanged. Thank you's were exchanged. Ethereal desires were transacted on the psychic plane. And me, I was out-a-there. Into my room, two-o'clock naptime.

I lay there, falling asleep. Believing I had found the perfect dream creature, sub-angel. No, not the receptionist, but the Chinese lady. You know, the one with the umbrella, ridin' shotgun on the back of that bike; *en route* to finish up with her college finals. The receptions was an ego back up—a just in case. The little girl; also a perfect goddess. But, she was two years from the harvest.

I nodded out. I caught some Z's.

As life would have it, as life usually does, I woke up in a state only life could produce—hard-on, full-on desire in the making. My dick was rock solid. But, a female body, such as it were, was nowhere to be found. Not yet anyway. So me, I instructed the bad pup to go down.

I got up. I washed my bones in the shower. The cold cement floor again chilled my feet. I prepared for the night.

After my shower, I sat for a moment. A moment in the over-all scene of the universe. I opened my creative notebook. I wrote love poetry to a woman—a Chinese/Burmese woman who I did not even really know.

Such is the life of the dreamer. Such is the life of a fool.

*   *   *

I played my time right. I planned to slide on out an hour or so ahead of the appropriate meeting time. You know, the time where I was to be accompanied to dinner by my beautiful Chinese/Burmese lady and her school-hood friends. The friends, I could give two fucks about. Her, on the other hand... Well, her...

So me, I planned to slice my way on up to the bar section and or area of the hotel. Seduce myself into the appropriate mode of illusion, via the alcohol. Maybe lay a bit of the rap on the sweet receptionist at the desk and then live. Yes, live. Live in my home; the night. The night that was oh so appropriately at hand.

Out I went; checked out the reception booth—nobody but the smiling male reception at hand. *Chill on dude...* Me, I headed up to the bar.

As I approached the door, I noticed a sign hanging on the wall saying, *"No one hundred-kyat notes accepted."* My mind passed over this, thinking it must be because they don't have enough change or something. But, post my second large scale brewski; while attempting to pay for the next round, I was told, to the effect, that the usage of these monetary implements of destructive currency had been shut down by the government; the *hundred-kyat* notes that is. The bad bartender dude, who had remembered me from my last time around Burma way, said, *"It was the government's way to hurt the Chinese, who had too much money in Burma anyway."* Chinese, the great entrepreneurs...

I guess this is as good as place as any to explain to you the relationship between the Chinese and the indigenous Burmese. In plain words, the Burmese don't dig 'em. Why? Well, it is based in the entrepreneurial spirit of Chinese. What goes on, and has gone on for generations/for centuries, is that the Chinese relocate; show up with money in their pocket. They then set up shop. And, they make more money; local money. Now, this goes on not just in Burma but all across South and Southeast Asia. So, they are non-too-loved; at least not by the locals. The locals don't dig their raking in the cash and then flaunting their wealth in their faces. So, in places like Burma, they periodically do things like shut down the currency; i.e. no more *hundred-kyat* notes.

That's the story… Back to the barkeep.

Now this conversation; the conversation between him and I, transpired due to the fact, one *hundred*-kyat notes was all I had. Remember, I had just changed the AMEX, (American Express), *don't leave home without 'em,* traveler's checks into local Burma *kyat*, pronounced, *"Chat."*

Me, being the mega cool traveler, (not tourist), that I am, I did not push the issue. I scraped together the minor small bill change that I had from my currency exchange, sat down, and me; I drank another round.

I slammed this one down hard and fast. The way only a true nirvana drinker can do. Then, I proceeded downstairs to gain understanding, knowledge, and possible enlightenment as to just what the fuck was going on with the money situation.

Upon the downstairs decent, I could see the droves of tourists, (not travelers), all onslaughting the front-and-central desk, wanting answers; desiring their money back, and all those bullshit things that a only tourist would do.

There was even an *expat* or two stalking the money exchange. British probably. They looked British.

I don't know, maybe after they had spent time in Burman during their military service; maybe they feel in love with Mandalay. Or, maybe it was a woman—a Burman woman. Maybe, I don't know. But, there they were. In need of a transition of money, as well. But, I could tell, they were in the same, *"Good luck,"* category as everybody else.

Me, I slide to the side—gave my sweet young Burmese *thAng* the eye; for she was back at the desk, listening to all the tourist and *expat* bullshit. She looked back at me. Our eyes/our glance met in a realm of perfection. I think it was then I knew that she was mine. Mine for all eternity if I wanted her. Well, such as all eternity is.

She immediately walked to me, avoiding the loud mouths of the massive others. We even kind of laughed when I said, *"No, I didn't care if the desk had enough of bills to exchange my one hundred-kyat notes for the smaller and simper versions."*

You see, there was only a certain, defined and designated amount, that this government run hotel had set aside/had been given for the exchange/retrieval of those big bills. The bills they had actually disked out to the people—like in my case, just a few hours before.

Me, I have long known; smaller is simpler. But then, smaller and simpler has never been my *thAng.*

To cover my backside, I exchanged some U.S. hundred-dollar bills, into the smaller denominations of the Burmese *kyat.* They were, of course, happy to do that—put some U.S. hundred-dollar bills in their coffers.

I mean like hey, who's foolin' who? They didn't want those big one *hundred-kyat* notes either.

53

For with a government like the one that runs Burma, they, (the hotel), didn't even know if they would ever be able to exchange them. So, they weren't kickin' too much of their bucks loose for the exchange, if you catch my meaning; and I think that you do. But, that old U.S. hundred-dollar bill, now there they had some *kyat* to exchange for it.

Yeah, I had bucks back then—didn't even care about the few hundred I had dropped. *"Time to kill and money to spill,"* that was my slogan. That was far before this time—now, currently, as I write these pages.

*   *   *

We spoke, Nanda Soe and I, as the crowds continued to congregate. We discussed politics, life, spirituality, her, and I, and all of the things that add up to nothing—not a goddamned thing at all.

I told her I was *en route* to having dinner with a group of college students that I had met during the day. She asked me if I was, would be available tomorrow, early morning—to go to her temple with her. And, like a gift from the grace of the hands of God, which I have always been so blessed to receive, I accepted her invitation. I accepted the chance. *With every dance there is another chance.*

If I can side note, sidetrack, side bar here for just half a second. People often wonder/question why I like the deep and dark realms of out-back Asia so much. Well, if you look at the amount of forever love that has been poured at my feet and the experiences lived in such a short amount of time. Well, the answer is obvious.

*   *   *

We, Nanda Soe and I, stared into each other's eyes for a moment or three. Then, one of my friends arrived. The main dude. The blue button-up shirt dude—still wearing his blue button-up shirt. The one who had actually made the invite to make plans for this endeavor.

I left Nanda Soe to deal with the droves of the tourists, the *expats,* the fools, who believed that you could put a price tag on experience; a dollar sign, or *kyat* sign, such as it were, on freedom. Fools, the lot of them. As most, they never had any idea how to live.

As I proceeded out of the main entrance of the hotel; a large open, straightened arch type of exit. I was curious, for there is/was, only one. Where were all of the rest of my soul lads and lasses? Is he actually planning to try to jack me? Am I going to have to kick some serious ass? I mean, let's be real; it has been tried before. Always to their dismay. The dismay and loss of the other(s). They never should have tried!   But, that is another/other stories and tales.

He led me on, into the night…

*   *   *

Outside the gate, the main gate, the protected gate; there they awaited. Probably due to all of the possible government type infractions and rules—no doubt due to hotel policy of keeping locals out, tourists in.

Smiles, hellos, were all around. There they were on their scoots, their rides, their cycles.

Pronounced, *"Cicles,"* by the locals. Burma bicycles to the max.

The crew had even picked up a few more riders of the night. A couple more dudes. To tell you who they were; they looked just like the other dudes. Short black hair; dark skinned.

The cycle mamas, the chicks, there numbers were the same: three.

The whys and wherefores, the discussion of how and who would ride each bike, took place. The main leader of the pack, head honcho; the one who had invited me/had come to get me; asked me if I could ride a bike. I smiled/I laughed, I told him that Stateside, I rode my bad Italian made bicycle average fifty miles a night; to keep in shape.

Well, in truth, that took some translating. But, I got the point across; that, *"Yes,"* I could ride.

It was up and down and all around, who would ride how, where and why. For a moment, the chick/my chick; the Chinese sub-goddess of my dreams, was to ride shotgun with me. But then, in all their trying to be nice, she hit the scoot of another.

We were off. Damn!

I had no idea where they planned to take me. As we peddled into the darkening coming winter night of Mandalay, we talked; such as we could. And then, came a memorable expression. Well, at least, a memorable expression to a dude with my mentality and nature—growing up in L.A.'s Southcentral and the gutters of Hollywood, and all... *"The Streets,"* in other word(s), to anyone of you out there who doesn't know where those places are or what they are like.

Anyway, this one new bike ridin' dude, whose introduction I had just made, over/outside of my hotel, sliced on by, as the cycling went on, and he said, *"Tonight we are going to have much good time."*

Now, to me, my mind instantaneously went to just what does this *Soul Cat* mean by that? Are we going to smoke some of that bad Burma hashish? Which, in fact, I had just recently done down in the capitol, Rangoon, with some locals. But, that's another story... Or, was it going to be a serious sex party session? Which I, in truth, would much prefer. My mind went to counting the numbers; four dudes, five counting me; three chicks. Me, I knew who I was going to be all over. And, no way, was anyone else going to touch her if I was *a-gettin'* busy.

But then, I began to wonder, as only a street kid can do, *"Does this go on all the time? Is she, just another one of those party sluts?"* Lord knows, I have known a lot of them... Intimately.

Anyway, that was indeed the internal ramblings of a fool, of a street kid, turned mystic. You know the type. Me.

We cruised maybe half a mile to a little restaurant, center stage/center Mandalay. Wooden by construction—windows open; lights on.

*   *   *

Sorry, you'll have to excuse me here. I have just taken a moment; actually more than a few moment(s), to further intoxicate myself with a touch of the grape—red wine; ten years, plus, old.

Excuse me, but I am more than a bit aced. I watched T.V. for a few. Boring T.V. I watched music videos; the craze of the late 80's in which I currently sit. And yes, it is true, but I wish I were in

Asia. Asia; anywhere in Asia. Anywhere but here and in psychological pain. Psychological pain; the poet's elixir.

The ocean waves outside, they ring in my ears. Home, such as it is. A $910.00 a month apartment. Yes, home. But, my dreams, my illusions; well, they lie in a world where the skin tone is not so white, the hair not so light, and the dreams; yes, the dreams, they are available for the taking. Excuse me, in my drunken ramblings. Now, I will get back to the story.

*   *   *

It was a place that I had seen before. Seen before, but never tasted the cuisine.

Inside, there were other(s). Other white folks. Some over here and a few over there. A group of four. No, not *the-gang-of-four,* for all you history aficionados. But, simply a group of four; probably German. I intentionally did not take extensive notice.

Inside, I did not feel, *The Special. The Special, The Only*—the feeling that I feel in Asia. That of, most commonly/most certainly, being the only white folk. But, times have unfortunately changed. The world has become open to the masses. The masses or, at least, the jet-set German hippies—which are the only ones who seem to travel to these remote regions.

Hippies, I don't like 'em.

Though my hair is long. But, the hair does not make the man.

Though there was a time... Yeah, way back when/then. Way back in the sixties and into the seventies, when they meant something... Then, not now.

Back then; me too. I wore love beads. Love beads when I was eight, nine, ten, thirteen years old. Love was in the air. San Francisco was the only dream in my mind. But, that was a long time ago.

*   *   *

Perhaps they planned, they thought, they assumed that there should be a basic debate as to what to eat. They wanted to discuss the subject with me. But, me... Yeah, well, me; I turned the tables. I handed over the reins of dinner deciding over to *the leader of the pack*. You know, the one guy. I gave him null-and-void priority on what to and wherefore to order. As food was the last thing on my mind.

*   *   *

Now, I suppose I could go into naming all the people I was with. This is, if I could remember their names. Which I can't. As such and because of, I think it would only make this stage of the story much more complicated and much more difficult to follow. So, I will try to just give you the basic definition(s) of the crew as necessary. From this, you will be able to, more easily, follow what is a-goin' on.

*   *   *

There she sat, that woman, that Chinese/Burmese sub-princess. My apparent dream of all the ages before and after all the ages had come and gone. Virgin, I believed her to be one.

Here, this is Southeast Asia. This is Burma. This is/she is, and she must be one. At least so I assumed…

She sat there directly across the table from me. It was a round table. Round and wooden. They, the proprietors, gave us a room to ourselves. A dining room. A small room. But, a room to ourselves none-the-less.

No Germans around. Just me and them. The locals from far off regions of Burma and me.

She stared at me. I at her. She mentioned, once again, how handsome I was. I commented, once again, how beautiful she was. And, if any dream were in the making, if any dream were worth a dime, I wanted her, I needed her. Dinner, it did not matter. Love, it is what I have forever been *a-seeking*. Seeking a form, just like hers.

After the main dude of the party ordered what he felt may be acceptable, what may be at hand, we sat back to enjoy our conversation.

Open parentheses:

(Again, may I make a note here? A note within parentheses; live the dream, all I can ever tell you is to live the dream. Whatever the price. Whatever the cost. Without it, in the end, your life will add up to nothing. Not anything at all.

Yes, it is true. I write these words under the influence of intoxication. But, here I sit. And, in all my life, the only thing(s) that have meant a goddamn—meant anything at all, were the dreams that I have been allowed to embrace on this physical plane of existence.

May I paraphrase/elaborate: two different words; different meanings, but subject to all that is

60

whole… And there, out there on the extremities, is the only place that dreams and literature may ever be formed).

Close parentheses:

The main function-or of the scene made the comment, post the comment of the babe, that stated, *"I was handsome."* He smilingly questioned, *"Did I like her?"*

"Yes, I did." What else could I say? The truth is, of course, the best weapon.

As the night and the conversation(s) continued; my mind, my body, my desire went to her. Could she be anything but mine?

*   *   *

Now Burma, and the people thereof, are perhaps left over from a different time—a different world. Or, at least, they base their influences upon the hearts and minds of their ancestors.

The main population of dudes, for example, have their arms, and other parts of their bodies fully *tatted* down, you know. Now, this is, of course, not the only and overall case but the numbers, especially those of the main population, are prodded and poked; inked up and down.

These associates which I had made friends with were, for the most part, rural folk coming to the biggest city they had ever seen, Mandalay. Which is not a big city by the standards of BIG at all. But, to them is was gigantic.

Anyway, these tattoos, of which I speak, did not have the highly evolved artistic techniques of say West Hollywood, Japan, or even the

Philippines. Instead, they were more of the neo-modern and/or of the primitive look. Anyway, the dudes I was *chillin'* with; well, they had *tats.*

The main leader of the pack, who sat next to me, to my right, had an arm full of 'em. I asked as to their origin. He pointed to one and said, with pure egotistic pride, that this was from his karate school. He said this while making the martial art style knife hand in the air. *"Oh, we had something in common,"* I thought. I inquired as to whether or not he was a black belt. He did not understand me and simply reiterated the fact, with pride, that it was from his karate school and then he flipped the old knife hand in the air again.

I had thought to tell him of my long involvement with the martial arts and the fact that I was a Master Instructor and had a school back in L.A. But, as words escaped definition, thereby any understanding at all; it all seemed worthless. And, for the most part, in general, I prefer to keep that part of my life more-or-less in the shadows anyway.

The inquiries were made as to if I was *tatted* down. No, I have none.

After a quick around the table, a time or three, complete with the flashing of this bad *tat* or that bad pup, the subjects changed—conversations changed. And, the meal was brought on.

We had, and or ate, your traditional type Burmese meal. A bit spicy; not so good/not so bad, in terms of the stimuli of the taste buds. He, the leader, kept trying to dish me up more grub. I got way too full.

Ages were exchanged. He, the head honcho, was twenty-five, only two years younger than I. And, two or three years older than the others at the table. I guess that is what put him in command.

My mind, being very inquisitive, as it tends to be, wondered why he would be a wee bit older than the rest—as they were all completing college at the same time. But, my question(s) never found their answer, due to linguist lackings.

In any case, one of the new *hombres* on the scene told me he wanted to come to my country. I told him America and Burma, were like night and day. It took some explaining around the table but the message finally got across.

The meal, though I suppose memorable in its own right—memorable enough to be writing about it here; was what it was. But, in reality, it was little more than that—a passing encounter into and onto the realms of oblivion; waiting only for someone such as I to become the illustrator in order to move it from its actually nothingness to the bounds of literary immortality.

Just for the record. The babe's eyes. The predominate one in my mind, were continually on me.

*   *   *

We were done. We had finished. I had expected to get stuck with the bill. In fact, I brought the cash to cover the folly.

I was more than surprised that when it came time to pay and the cool commandant of the crew insisted on picking up the tab. It had to cost him a pretty penny. A penny in Burmese fashion; such as it were. And in truth, I really was far better equipped at the handling of paying that pretty penny than he was. But, he insisted. AOK dude.

He had to snag a bit of small change from one of the other tattooed guys to cover the damage.

You know, the one who told me he wanted to come America's way.

Paid in full. We proceeded on out-a-there.

We had been sat in a bit of a private parlor, as I told you. Off to one side. Conveniently equipped with its own personal fan. All nice enough... *"Thank you,"* I tossed in the direction of the *maitre'd* as we rambled our way out-a-there.

As we waltzed towards and then out the door, I noticed all there were left inhabiting the space were locals. On our way in, as mentioned and detailed, there had been a few of the European guesthouse hippies within the establishment. I was glad to see they were all gone. For it really is my scene to be the one and only westerner in the works, if you know what I mean. But, anyway.

Outside, we got on our rides. The riding patterns were rearranged somewhat; post a bit of a discussion in Burmese. I had a new scoot, But, we were off, none-the-less. As we peddled, my mind kept going to the comment the dude had made earlier, *"We are going to have much fun tonight,"*

And me, being who I am; having lived the life I have lived, I was wondering where to next? Where to—to set this kid in the party mode.

As we drove through the streets, the conversation went on between them. Me, I was all smiles, being the mega bitch'n nice guy sort of dude that I am. The ride went on.

A turn—a corner like any other turn or corner. The kind we have all seen so many times before. But, this one came with a new sense of reality.

BLAM! SPLAT! POW! You know, like in the old Batman T.V. series. The girl, you remember the one; Burman with the bright red lipstick. Well, she had been riding shotgun on the backside of another. The other—a new dude who had come along for the free ride of a free meal. He was at the helm. She was riding bitch. He misjudged the corner—a little; a bit too much of a tilt. And then, the slip and the slide. They were down.

Perhaps it was not too gentlemanly of me, but I have always found it best to take humor into all of these situations. Me, I laughed. I laughed, hard and loud. They looked up. The crew, you know. The girl, a bit bloodied. Not at all amused.

I admit, I felt a little bad for laughing. But, come on… I would had laughed if I had chewed it.

Pulling themselves off the arching ground, they/we were again making our way. I did not like the signs of what I saw coming. We were heading back to my hotel.

We arrived. They stopped. Bid me all the goodbyes.

We all made plans for my intended return trip in three weeks, post a jaunt to Dacca. Then, after that, I was to head back to Burma, *en route* to home sweet far away from home, home, Bangkok.

I was told, I could find them all in Mandalay for the next few months. All, except the Chinese chill princess who was graduating, day next, and going home.

We bid our *adeus*. They rearranged bicycles. And, with dreamy eyes, she was off. Her, the babe, the potential woman who could answer all of my dreams.

Me, I was alone. The main maximum dude had made his point. He treated everyone to dinner. Mega points for the babes and his position of power and authority reconfirmed in his direction.

Me, I was dumbfounded. Where was the party I had been promised? Come-expect. But, gone. Out the window. Through the old door into the lost realms of a Burmese roll in the carpet that never happened. I was not happy. What could I say/what could I do? I looked at my watch. Fuck, it was only 7:45 in the P.M.

I went by the desk. My secondary main squeeze had checked out; punched out on the old time clock. No-go there either. I went into my room. I turned on the light. There was a giant sized black cricket sitting right on my fucking pillow. Now, I was really pissed. So, I picked it up. The pillow, that is. I threw the *mutha fucka* in the toilet and flushed it. I sat down in all my not getting my own way and with nothing I could do about it... I sat down and realized I was seriously love sick. A feeling, let me tell you, that I am not proud of.

I wrote a few lost love poems. Then, in no mood to sit and stare at the fading wallpaper walls, I took the incentive and made my move for the upstairs bar area with the intention of wetting my lips.

I hoped... One side of me did anyway, not to bump into the babes and the city slicker from the previous night. But, the other side wanted any remedy at hand.

For whatever karmic factor they were not there. So, I pounded me a few of the tall ones, hit on down the stairs and went to sleep elevenish.

Part III

Day three: I woke. It was the day to meet Nanda Soe. I had to set my bad little credit card size alarm clock/calculator; which I had picked up for my very first trip to India. I still have and use that bad pup to this day.

I needed it, for this was way too early for me. 7:30 AM wake up session, for an 8:00 AM rendezvous.

Yeah, I was up and out of the old sack, Jack. You know, it is one of those things with me, that if I wake up to an alarm, something which I hate to do, I have to bail the bedside in the mode of immediately or I will just roll over, chill back, and sleep until I awake, *au natural.* So, I forced myself. I was up/out.

I put on/wore my bad red Polo shirt. The one I didn't sell to all the entrepreneurs down Rangoon way. My way baggy brown pants with have pockets on the side, midway down. And, of course, my *Puma Power Cats.*

Now, Nanda Soe, she lived with her uncle down the street. She had given me the directions, verbally, and they sounded *no problema* to find.

Me, I waltzed out of my room; out of the hotel. I walked out into the day. The crystal blue Burmese sky; a white cloud, here/there, caught me, warm air embraced me, and I could not help but felt the touch of the goddess as she slowly caressed my soul.

Walk, yeah, I walked down the few blocks to the realms of no return. The house was on the right side of the street, just a block or two past the moat surrounding the palace. Number three, it was easy enough to find.

I walk up the path and there she sat, out in front; Nanda Soe, awaiting my arrival. Seated upon a bench. A bench out in the yard.

The house was basically a pretty cool crib. Not on the *econo* side of the picture. No, not at all. She greeted me. She invited me in and gave me the look-see.

To enter, we walked past your basic, give the tourists a ride, open in the back, type of tourist truck. A rare site; being personally owned and all, here in Mandalay. Past that, past the porch, into the living room, there sat a modern and way cool, on a black, high tech side of the picture, color T.V. and a VCR down below. I kinda had to laugh, for I mean like there is no reception in the T.V. department in Mandalay. And video, well, I hadn't seen any video stores.

The dude, her uncle, the guy the house belonged to, obviously had to be on the big bucks fridge of the Southeast verging on the South Asian side of the picture.

Then he, her uncle, struts on into the room. Nice guy, I guess. Dark skinned, fiftyish, graying hair, sprouting a modern western tee-shirt with some American T.V. show title radiating across the front of it. He spoke near perfect English and was quite proud of the fact that tourists liked him so much that they recommended all of their future oncoming tourist friends to him as their guide.

Nice guy, yet there was something— something that projected something more than a tourist guide vibe about him. I was not quite sure what it was. You know, you just don't get those kinds of bucks guiding tourists. At least not in

Burma. That is unless you guide them to a certain type of place, or should I say a certain type of feeling.

Well anyway, I will leave that to your imagination, as I have no real proof.

He informed me that Nanda Soe had been waiting for me since 7:00 AM. Hey, I rap'd to the cat that I was not set for rendezvous central until 8:00 in the A.M. Told him, didn't even get out of the sac, Jack, until 7:30. But then, the babes do love to wait for me. Why, I do not know? But anyway...

With intros out of the way, we were Out-a-Dodge. Me, Nanda Soe and I. Our sights set on some temple in the distance. Where she, Nanda Soe went to meditate daily. A lot of people in Burma— those of the spiritual persuasion do just the same.

Out on the streets, we walked a bit; then hit over for this local food stall. Now, as mentioned, the sky was blue, the streets, paved and unpaved, the houses wooden by structure and nature, the people dark skinned, the weather warm. But, fuck me, wouldn't you know it, she pulls us into this dive of a local greasy spoon, with dirt on the floor, dirt on the wooden tables, plastered walls, covered with dirt, a low and dark ceiling, made with what looked to be straw, (as there was still some hanging loose), and people, way too many people. But, this was her world. What could I say/do? We sat down.

She ordered up her preferred poison. And, they did sling the hash. It was this kind of weird *poi* thing—kinda tasted like goop made out of sour flour. They also threw in this *chapati* sore of *tortilla thAng* that they fried in this obviously dirty pan. Then, they poured us what looked to be local java for a drink.

Happy? Well no, not too... I expected to get sick as a *mutha fuckin'* dog. But, being the gentleman that I am, what could I say?

I had no choice but to eat it. Overall, the taste wasn't too bad. I have eaten way worse out on the outskirts of the far-off realms.

Post that little local encounter, we were off and onto the street again. We had walked a few, when up comes this bus, and that was what we were supposed to motor forward on.

*   *   *

I don't know... Let me go into a little bit of an explanation here.

It's not like I'm not continually up for new and different experiences. I mean, that is why I go to the Asian side of the tracks continually—in quest of experience. But, as this day progressed, I kept getting the slap of the unexpected. The unexpected that I didn't want to expect. In fact, I had no idea what was to come next. I mean like, when I was invited to a temple, you know, I expected something in city and local—not a bus ride out onto the fringes of eternity on the outskirts of Hades.

Anyway... I got on the bus.

Now this bus, forget that it was bumpy, no shocks to the max. But, it was just not designed for *homeys* like myself—those of us being over the six-foot mark.

I mean, that is not all that tall by modern standards, you know. But, in Burma, it is/I was massive.

I mean like, first I had to seriously bend down to enter that bad back door. But, being *The Back Door Man* that I am. Like you know, *"The men don't know, but the little girls; they understand."* Then, I had to like, keep the bend going on to make it to the seat, 'cause the ceiling was way too low for me to stand up.

Well, I made it to the seat; where we, Nanda Soe and I, sat for a time. Now, that was still and basically AOK. That was until the bus started to mega fill up and I, being the gentleman that I am, relinquished my seat to some local miss, who looked like she needed it, way far more than me.

So, there I stood: bouncing, humping, and thumping; in like a bend over position. Next, to add insult to injury, the bus became more full-on crowded. Too full for my claustrophobic nature to feel comfortable at any level. So, I had to bail for the back. The back, where people were now hanging on from the rear door. Me too.

Everybody was all smiles and all that sort of stuff. Sure… No doubt, dude… It had to be pretty fucking funny to see this longhaired blonde white boy, bouncing down the highway in Burma, with all of the locals, as he held on for dear life. Held onto the back door, onto the bus ladder, onto the roof railing that held the people and the people's shit up topside of this bad form of mass transit.

In fact, and in truth, I lost my grip more then once and almost went flying. Plus, this was no short and/or direct ride. This *mutha fuckin'* journey took time.

Then, as now, it kind of reminded me of this one time when my bud, Saturday Jim and I; along with this other bro, from back in the day, Mad Mike and his wife; cruised up North to the mountains above Bakersfield.

I think I was sixteen. S.J. seventeen. And, M.M. and his wife, eighteen. Anyway, I cruised them and I, in my ride, up to the mountains to visit Mad Mike's dad.

Now, Mad Mike was way into the LSD. One of those dudes who had just done way too much of it. Done it, even though he was a *Born Again Christian.* He had all kinds of excuses and justifications about how and why it was okay for him to continue to take said drug, even though it was totally against his church. But, I won't bore you and go into all of that.

Anyway, up there, in the mountains, we were cruising along this dirt road, in the back of the Mad Mikes father's, friend's old junky pickup. The guy, AWOL from the Navy. But basically, an AOK sort of dude.

Oh yeah, MM's father was a way burnt out old hippie; deep in his fifties, with a thirteen-year-old girlfriend. Thirteen, no lie…

Anyway, we're cruising along this back road and *Bam,* we hit a massive bump. Me, I went flying. What was funny is that I didn't even feel it until I landed, feet first, on the road. There I was, fully standing, as they drove on. One of my crew, ridin' shotgun in the back, had to tell the drivin' dude to stop; to let me climb back in. Life huh…

Well anyway, I didn't go flying from the bus in Burma, but it was close call more than once.

And, like every time someone would climb up to the topside, to either plant themselves or some object of food or possession on the roof, I had to chill back and let go of my now safely revered position of grip and hold onto the upward bound bus ladder; which was not near as secure.

Finally, we made it way far out and into the countryside. There she came, Nanda Soe, pushing her way through the crowded bus. We got off.

Though it was a kill adventure. In fact, more feelings encountered than could ever be expressed in words... None-the-less, I was more than happy to get off that *mutha fuckin'* bus at the temple sight central.

*   *   *

We walked, Nanda Soe, and I. We strolled down a dusty trail flanked by vegetation found, indigenous, only to this region. We spoke of the ride, of the day, of the Buddha. We spoke until we found our way to the temple—which one would not even know was there; if they did not know, that it was there.

It was in the back; deep, almost hidden, behind the growths of nature.

Now, here we are, at this off-white, Southeast Asian, not so clean, temple of the Buddhist sect. It did not have the neon glowing, vibrating in disco form, halo of rings pulsating around the head of the Buddha, as say the ones did, down Rangoon way. Simple. It was differently simpler.

Nanda Soe showed me around the place. And then, she strategically placed me upon a cement bench under a Southeast Asian tree, over to one side of the temple. She never asked if I wanted to come in and chill my bones in the various forms of meditation. She just assumed I did not.

She handed me a book. She walked on. She walked in.

I was left sitting with a book titled, *"Burma."* You know, one of those basic tourist guides.

It had an inscription in it. Obviously given to her uncle. *"Thank you for all the insight you gave us in Burma. See you again."*

Well, fuck me! I did not know quite what I had expected once I got here. But, sit here with a book that I don't want to read. Well, fuck me.

The bus ride, yeah, that was an adventure in itself. But, there I sat in all of my alone. Who knows how long that she will take a-sitting in lotus position?

I sat there, tried to chill. I stared off into space. The space of space. You know the type, very Zen and all.

Moments cast to the reflection of the nothing.

Yeah, once I had only dreamed of being in such a place. Meditating in the *holy* that Asia is supposed to hold. And, there I was, years later; years after I was a *Brahmacharya*, then a *Swami*.

Yeah, like it is all just a game, you know. A game of what uniform that you wear. A game of who is high, who is low, who is holy, or who is not.

Awh, but you can read some of the other books of mysticism that I have written if you really want to get way more into my realizations of/and about that… Here, this is a story about life. What is lived. What is known. What is felt. What is whatever. Call it what you will…

So me, I sat there. I tried to keep a self-actualized opinion about the whole thing. Tried to drink it all in: the picture, the scene, and the movement of the big ant on my bench. Fuck it! I didn't want to get bit by that son of a bitch that kept coming my direction. I killed it with the book. Bap!

Post that; with nothing better to do, I read through the book a bit. Read about the different ethnic stocks that make up this political territory known as Burma. I read, I dreamed, and yeah, I did think about my Chinese chill princess who was by now, no doubt, on her way back to her land in distant Burma. The land where she came from. The place where no white traveler was supposed to travel to.

As I sat, some little local homey; maybe seven or eight years of age, came and checked me out. He stood there and stared for a few. No biggy... I smiled.

Then, I sat. I waited. There in the temple court yard of *Burma Mata.*

Finally, maybe an hour or three into the session, when I was seriously thinking about seeing if I could figure out the bus route and bail my way back to Mandalay, out she came; Nanda Soe—none the worse for the wear.

She sat down and we began to speak about the nothing that people are continually interested in. I told her of how I once sat, daily, in the position; full lotus and all, and focused on the thought of nothingness; in search of higher paths/higher thoughts. But then, I realized that they were goals just the same. Goals that defeated the entire purpose. The purpose of no desire. I realized that were just another dose of the ultimate illusion; that there is no illusion at all.

Yes, just like the yuppies set a goal for themselves; guiding themselves towards mega power and position. But, meditating is supposed to be/claimed to be, so much more; so much more holy. For it is a goal to rise above the foolish and materialistic minds of the masses. Yet, a desire is just a desire. Don't let any of the so-called holy, fool you. They are just the same as you: desire-full.

So yeah, now my meditation is with my eyes open. Far more to learn and see that way. And oh yeah, speaking of eyes...

"What is it Nanda Soe? What is the pain that I see in your eyes?"

Yeah, you know, like it wasn't just rap I was dishing. There was this confusion, this discomfort that could be seen—seen in her eyes. It was almost like the eyes of someone who is about to enter into to the altered realm of psychosis or something. Her large eyes were deep, distant, tragic.

"Yes, Samuel. I am upset. There is this man. He is married but he likes to be with me."

As I am not really in the mood to go into this little *convo.* Words for word; play by play. I mean like, what the fuck difference does it make anyway? So, I am just going to give you the overview basics. And, oh yeah, by the way, with her confession of a love stallion in tow, there went my vestal virgin dream of being the first to plant the mighty pup in the hoe. Yeah, that dream/desire went straight out the window of that old temple, near which we sat.

So, as he rap goes; she was twenty-eight, a year older than I was at the time. She had latched onto this love squeeze, for who the fuck knows what reason, and she had done the old get popped, get fucked continually, at the beckon call of his local fortyish love punk with his dick in a sling dude. And, like woe man, from this and because of this, she, like, got all way confused.

Hey, we all bake our own bread. I've heard the same story from a million different women; a different flavor, but the same taste, you know.

So, that was why she was a-meditating. To gain the strength to tell the dude to basically fuck off.

Me, I play the rap game…

"Oh, let me take you away to America."
"Anywhere would be fine but here," she answers.

Yeah right, just what I need, some babe latched up on the love potion number nine of some other homeboy. But anyway, deal me any hand, I will play it. And so, I put the old LOVE rap, full-on into motion. She bought it. Or maybe, it was me who fell for the old love-line again. I do not know who was playin' who.

In any case… She leaned forward and slapped some lips upon my mouth.

Hey what's a guy like me supposed to do?

So, it was the old basic one thing that led to the other and the other and the other, you know, I've written about it so many times in so many place before.

And yes, right there, in the foreboding shadows of holiness. Just outside the temple and Buddhist shrine. Yeah me, post her lips meeting mine; well, I lifted the old wrap around skirt, to reveal no underwear. And yeah, I did grab a bit of the sparsely haired snatch and small handful of her little, on the small boob side of the picture, breasts.

AOK in the AOK sense of the love stuff. And, well yes, I did plant the power pup home. She quickly got off. I got off. And that, my friends, was that.

A very small reaction to the ever-changingness of space, of time, of religion, and of truth. Nothing really. No, not to me. Just another moment that would be completely lost to the sands of time if it were not for this piece of literature.

I don't know... I guess it was just her way of reaching out; trying to find out if other men found her attractive. If she was attractive. If other men, once inside of her, made her feel the way that one dude it.

Well, all I got to say to that punk is, move over *mutha fucka*, believe me, I am sure you don't know how to fuck as good as I know how to fuck; even when, and if, it is orchestrated upon a bench in the shadows of a temple of holiness.

So, if nothing else, she knew/realized she was desired. Knew that another man could make her cum. She now knew this/now understood; if nothing else...

Post and after, she and I, we headed out for the outside—down the dirt path; through the archway that led from the temple to the road. We rode back into the city. Cruised to the city on another bus. Zero equaling only and nothing more than zero. Zero in a zero world.

The bus ride was way far less crowded in reverse. So, I got to plant myself on the seat next to her for the whole ride. It just was as it was; no biggy.

Mostly, what I was feeling is that whole, *"Why bother feeling."* Like, what was it all worth— what does it all mean. You know like, the desire, the conquest, the have/the had, and all of that. It just added, as it always seemed to do, up to the nothing at all.

I have to admit, however, that I have always wished, that it did mean something/anything more.

So back to the city. I walked her back to her crib.

She didn't have to be at work for a time. But me, I turned down the invite to come to the inside, and/as such, I walked on. I chilled on back to my abode. I passed the guy at the desk. Gave him the old thumbs up. And, into my room I went.

I lay there thinking/realizing that around every corner there was a new promise of love everlasting for me. For me; Burma-way, this time. A promise for the passion; the passion of love. Love, a passionate promise that never seems to last. A promise, none-the-less. And yes, these promises did suck me in. They did make me believe in the possibilities. Around every corner there seemed to come a new one. Hell, just when I was getting into the forever fantasy of one, I would blink, and a new one was being ushered in my direction. I wish all life was like this.

I lay there on the bed realizing that I had been hittin' a lot of unexpected pussy in Burma. Hittin' it, this time around. I was happy that my dick had been getting' wet. I lay there wishing that it all had meant/had added up to something/anything more.

I lay there thinking/wishing that she, Nanda Soe, would have been all that this fool had dreamed of. But, she was not. And thus, I felt like a tramp for playing the game once again. Another notch on the old dick and all...

Just zero… It all meant, *just zero.*

The thought of Kyi Hlaing came to mind. Oh yeah, that was her; the Chinese girl via a distant spot in Burma. Yeah, that was her name. I don't think I told you that?

But anyway, her thought continued to come to my mind. The pounding poison of the disease of love. Infatuation for the unknown. Infatuation, of and for the dreamed of/the hoped for.

Yeah, her and I; it was like some connection had been made. At least so I believed.

Sure, I danced around with the thought/with the idea that it could all just be based in the psychologically rooted problem of just being full-on tempted by the temptation of this babe of a creature. And yeah, you know, we all desire what we desire. Me, I love the ladies...

And then, there was the thought that maybe she was not all that her illusion promised to be. I mean like, look at old Nanda Soe. But, I couldn't shake it. So, post writing a lost love poem or thirty for her, I set about to write her a love letter. Yeah, I told her all about the fact that she was full-on the most intense babe that I had ever met and that she was the kind of woman which I had been seeking for all of my life, and all of that other type of love sick bullshit.

I guess, I probably still have the original copy of that letter somewhere. Somewhere, sitting lost in my creative travel notebook for that journey. You see, I always have at least two notebooks with me. One for the journalistic, diary type of entries; documenting life for posterity and all. And then, the creative one. The one for the poetry, the songs, and yeah even the love letter type of stuff.

Now that I think of it, I think that was the last love letter I have ever written. To date, anyway... And, I am sure, that is the last time I ever felt lovesick.

So anyway, I wrapped that bad puppy up in an envelope and headed for the desk to gain some bad homeboy to translate the English into Burmese on the envelope, to be sure that it would get to her.

I was glad to see that Nanda Soe had not arrived for her nightly, night shift, as of yet. So, no explanations asked for; none necessary.

My friend with the smiles, at the desk central, directed me into the office for what he felt was a better translator than himself. In, I went.

There was this fully Chinese guy in there. As it turned out, he was apparently the owner or manager or something of the hotel. Yeah, I guess the Chinese did have the country financially by the balls.

The government did attempt to fuck 'em, by pulling the old one *hundred*-kyat notes. But, how much damage did it do? I do not know?

The action taken was what it was. But, what was it? I mean, fuck, the world is what? One third Chinese bloodline, in terms of overall population. So, I guess that that they have earned, through procreation, if nothing else, their right to a certain influence.

But anyway... Back to the story.

Also, in there was this dude. A dude of obvious South Asian bloodline. He fully spoke good English and post a bit of the old figuring out; he did pen the address into Burmese. I mailed it off. Went on back to my room.

I lay there staring at the ceiling. Trying to figure out a way to forget Kyi Hlaing. Forget her, at least until there was the possibility of remembering her. Yeah, I lay there thinking that tomorrow was my day to bail on and down, via aircraft, to Pagan. Would I/could I find another/any other reason to just dream, to forget.

Yes, my seven-day visa would be up soon. There was little time that I had for healing—for finding another Burma dream worth dreaming.

I thought about the Chinese whores/the late-night princesses. You remember the ones. Maybe I could chill one of their bones tonight; if only they would show up at the upstairs hotel bar. But, maybe not... I couldn't count on it.

Then, there was Nanda Soe. Awh, forget that! I had already dipped my cookie in that once today. And, it really meant a whole lot of *nada*. I, for damn sake sure, didn't need to reinforce that feeling of sexual emptiness.

So, I lay there in bed, seeking a reason to rise. Watching my fan spin on the ceiling. I lay there desiring a reason to move. There was none.

Finally, in the late afternoon, it hit me. The reason for life. The reason for purpose. The reason for all of the paradoxes of the mystic's dream.

I got up and headed for the front—for the office that I had been in before. You know the one; the one that housed the guy who had translated the address for me.

Yeah, the office... It was the home of Tourist Burma in Mandalay.

Oh, for all of you uninitiated, the Tourist Burma Office is the only place that non-locals, like yours truly, can/could book passages to other reaches of their country.

"I want to go to Keng Tung."
"But, Mr. Slam, that is in a restricted region. You can't go there."

For you basic geography buffs, Keng Tung is a fair sized city in Eastern Burma. It is about equal distance from the China, Laos, and Thai borders. Being far into the heart of the *Golden Triangle,* (and we all know what goes on there), it was fully off limits to westerners. But, I was in no mood to take, *"No,"* for an answer.

"Now, I know that they have an airport there, because this address which I have is on Airport Road. I want to fly there. Sell me a ticket."
"We cannot do that Mr. Slam."
"Why, if they have an airport?"

Now, I won't bore you here with all the details. But, it was no-go by any means, dude. No-go due to all the government restrictions and the etcetera. They just couldn't do it. Couldn't sell me a ticket, no matter how much U.S. currency I offered them.

"How else can I get there?"
"You can't go there Mr. Slam."
"Okay, look... If you were going to go there, how would you get there?"
"I would fly."
"If you couldn't fly?"
"Then I guess that I would take a bus."
"Where would you catch the bus?"
"Downtown."
"Okay, fine. Thank you."

That was that. I had my destination, mode of transportation, and reason for the journey in mind. Oh, did I mention that is where Kyi Hlaing lived.

Hell, I had her address. What more of an invitation did I need?

Yeah, I had all preliminaries necessary. All the prerequisites, but not a fucking idea in hell how I was going to put the pedal to the metal and get my bad self where I knew I needed to be.

I went back to my room and let the hours of the night pour down on me in all of their Mandalay silence. I lay in my bed. I lay awake, digging for the courage and will of purpose to push forth and forward, to find my way to dream-land, in the arms of Kyi Hlaing.

Part IV

Wake up to the lack of no sleep, on the far side of midnight. Yeah, it was approximately six in the A of M. Awoken by my bad little credit card size alarm clock. You know the one.

I pulled my shit together a bit. Hit the hard and cold of the cement floor; drained the old lizard and hit the shower in all of its yellow water glory.

Done and through; a peek outside to see what the day had in store for me. Yes, the same: clear, sunny, and warm.

I would have headed for the bail right then and there, but the morning was young, the hotel restaurant not even open. No, not yet. So, I doubted if I could pay my tab and book for the white line/main line of the highway East.

Oh yes, did I tell you that my plan was set: fuck the restriction, fuck the rapidly ending seven-day visa, fuck it all. I had a destination in mind. Yeah, a destination to the arms of my dream and full-on hoped for lover. Obsession(s), they do take hold...

*   *   *

What to do as the early morning hours pass into the oblivion of one leading forward into/onto the next? I was filled full-on with all the fantasized anticipation of what moment/what causation was to stir next.

What. Is the answer.

I stared off into the hotel walls. Focused on the white sheets of my unmade bed. Peered into all of the nothing that makes up the something. Into all of the fantasies that leads one forward into all of the realms of this illusion; this illusion that we call life.

As the Buddha so eloquently put it, *"The cause of suffering is desire."* Here I was in this land of the Buddha. And yes, I was so eloquently dancing into a mega full-on desire. A desire, that once it began, there was no way to ever stop it or forgetting what occurred because of it; for doing that would be like way impossible.

*   *   *

The time had come. Yes, there would be someone at the pay to play, behind the, *Get-Out-a-Dodge* desk. My bag in hand, I waltzed forward.

Since I was to pay with credit card… I mean like fuck! They, the powers that be, had jacked all around with my carrying change. You know what I'm talkin' about. I mean like, I was still packing several of the old *hundred*-kyat notes that I couldn't use. So, who knows what's going to happen with the country's financial notes next. So anyway, enough of making a long story long…

I hit up to the desk. They sent me to the office of the previously mentioned Chinese dude, owner/operator. He was kickin' back and chilling behind his desk. He sprouting his loose and casual, short sleeve, white print shirt. I was met with the basic,

"Hello, Mr. Slam. Oh, you want to use your American Express to pay for your bill?"

You see, not like a commercial hype or anything, but in 1985 American Express was the only credit card that was accepted in Burma. As I write these pages, it still is to-day. Only now, the country is under *marshal law,* and like the travelers are not allowed to go mobile anywhere solo. One must have a guide.

In fact, if that were not the case, I would probably pack my bag and head on back there right now—upon completion of this text. But, that is just not my way to travel. No guide for me. Anyway...

"Oh, you have a platinum card. I have heard of these but I have never seen one before. They are the best card, yes?"
"Yes."
"I don't think that we can accept it."
"Why?"
"Well, we don't have the right forms and no one has told me what to do with them."

Well, fuck me. Like, I mean, a card is a card, right? But, anyway...

"How about this one?"

I pull out my lower level AMEX gold card.

"Yes, now this one I have seen a few times before. I know that we can accept it."

So, that was that. Fuck that dude too. Good thing I held onto the possession of the old gold card. I mean like, I had been promoted to the upper echelon realms of platinum but it wouldn't have worked. So much for the power and the glory of AMEX. Stupid, huh?

He processed me up. Told me of how he had not visited America as of yet but had been on down the European way.

Funny, I thought... All of the Southeast, verging on the South Asian, local poverty of this country and a non-local dude of the Chinese bloodline, moves on in and chokes up the change to the degree that he can travel to far off places and make a journey that none of the locals even have the dream of doin'. Damned, if that ain't the story of this world.

"I am glad that you have decided to go onto Pagan, as you had previously intended and not to Keng Tung. But, why are you checking out so early, the truck to the airport doesn't come for several hours?"
"Just want to view a little more of your beautiful city."
"Oh, I understand."

Yeah, right.

So, I bid *adieu* to the Mandalay Hotel. No one the wiser for where I was planning to trek.

I sliced a wave of, *"Asta,"* to the bad soul boy at the desk with a smile. And no, Nanda Soe, had not arrived yet.

As I was leaving, I noticed that sitting/leaning against one another, out on the curb, in front of the hotel, was this cute couple that I had met at the Tourist Burma Office in Rangoon. They were Canadian, via Vancouver way.

Yeah, Saturday Jim and I did have our kicks up there more than a few times in our teens and early twenties. In fact, we had it down to a science—a drive, Hollywood to Vancouver, nineteen hours. So, I immediately held a certain affinity for the couple. He was blond, styling a short cropped *'do.'* She was pretty, had red hair, a bowl cut.

As I had been told, from Rangoon they had planned to go first to Pagan, then to Mandalay, via a rented diver in a rented jeep. As it turns out, on their way from Pagan to Mandalay, (the actual distance is only about a hundred and fifty miles or so), well it, the jeep, had a problem—kinda crapped out. So, they were left with no further way to proceed. The driver, cool enough, set them up on a local bus to get them rest of the way to Mandalay.

The bus ride, as you can imagine/as previously depicted in my case in point, went on down. It was probably none-too-fun.

Anyway, they had pulled in late with no place left to run. They were fully tired of the guesthouse style accommodation(s), out house in the back and all, as they had done down in Pagan. They wanted to chill more seriously. So, they had tried to catch a room at the hotel here. But, there was none available—as the story goes/as can be expected. So, there they sat; leaning against one another all night.

I smile. Isn't love grand?

Now, as much as I would have liked to sit around and shoot the shit with 'em, I was a man with a mission. I was in the mode of bail.

I told them that I had just checked out, so there was a room available. And, if they wouldn't give it to them to wait for Nanda Soe to arrive and drop this kid's name, Samuel Slam, on her. I was certain that she would set 'em up.

Whether it was true or not, I didn't really know. But I tried…

I strutted my bad stuff down the street, left in the direction of the down-of-town. The sun was still hidden to the sights of the horizon. The Royal Palace, Mandalay Fort, surrounded by its moat, was emanating the silence of power and control.

Yeah, over there, to my shoulder, right; the sky, placid blue, like an awakening in the realms of the land where only a Buddha may survive. My body, it began to sweat, as the heat sliced another notch from my soul.

Past the Palace, two blocks up, third house on the right. I had a destination in mind. The house of the old uncle of Nanda Soe.

I approached it—the house that is. I knew Nanda Soe would be in the mode of meditation at the temple. She had told me, that on this day, it would be her AM destination. As it is every day. I wondered, if this time, she would be meditating upon the love of sexuality that I had given her in the shadows of holiness.

You remember her story? Her mind of love attempting to run away from the dude who only wanted to do her/use her. Leaving her broken/fractured/shattered.

How fucking typical is that story in the annals of life? How many millions of times has it been lived out?

Anyway, it wasn't her in which I was interested. I had already had her/done her; just like the old dude. But, I am certain, I had done her a hell of a lot better.

We, her and I, had been as close as two human beings can be on this physical plane. Yes we had.

Sad, I guess. I was just like him; the dude who first grabbed her brain, absorbed her love.

Took it/used it; only to spit it out. But, me... I am based in a completely different realm of reality. Yes, sex, is the outcome of the desire. But sex, is not the end-all. It is simply the pathway to the literature of enlightenment. For with every new woman, every new touch, there is new a deeper realization about the cosmic nature of existence.

Perhaps... At least I hope, her mention in this writing and your reading, will all equal something more than nothing. And, the karma will be cleansed/released/forgiven. Perhaps? I do not know.

*   *   *

Anyway, having had it/done it, that was not what I was there for. Me, I needed a method; a guide if you will. And, there was only one guide that I knew.

I knocked. He answered.

"I need to get to Keng Tung."

With a laugh,

"Why do you want to go there?"
"There is someone there which I need to see."
"Why do you need to see someone there? I am sure that we could fill all of your needs, here locally."

Hint, hint...

Now, as I don't want to bore you with the particulars of conversation, as some writers do, I will just give you basics.

Me, I wanted the bad lad to take me mobile in his bad little tourist type truck—wanted him to drive me straight to the doorway of my princess of dreams up there in Keng Tung.

I mean, the thought/the realization had come to me as I lay in my bed; evening last. I could see it. I could feel it. My driving, in all of my perfection, right up to the door of my desired babe—sweeping her off her, oh so fragile, virgin feet. Yeah, taking her away to the lost safe realms of a California beach city in America. You know, get a white picket fence and live happily ever after.

But, as fantasies never really do come true; at least not the way that you had them planned in your mind.

Oh by the way… Do you know why that is? That's because you always envision the most perfect event to happen. I know, I know, your logic kicks in now. *Well, isn't that a fantasy? The best of the best of what is available and offered?*

But me, for example, I used to try to envision the less than perfect outcomes, as well. The better than nothing outcome…

But, it is still all fantasy. And, a fantasy is a false reality.

And, because of, and the reality thereof; so far/thus far in my life, only once did what I fantasy come exactly into reality. I guess I was fourteen. But, that was a long time ago…

I guess the thing to take away from this storyline divergence is that in certain regards, once you have the fantasy, in a certain reality, it <u>is</u> lived, experienced, known.

Anyway… He, Nanda Soe's uncle, wouldn't drive me. He was worried about the, *"What if I get caught?"* And, all the etcetera. He even sliced in the question/statement,

"What about Nanda Soe and how much she loves you?"
"Hey dude, all the babes love this kid right here."

He just didn't want to go for the mobile session, you know. But, I wouldn't give in to the no-go.

Finally, after chocking up more then a bit of the old American cabbage, he agreed to take me and place me upon the proper bus headed towards Keng Tung. At least that was something.

We walked in the direction of the bus strop for the bus ride. The bad dude didn't want to pull his *short* out of the gay-rage, so we had to hoof it. Whatever...

Once we were there, where the buses take off from, we had to wait a bit. So, we chilled back in the warmth of the coming day had a local tea. *"Cha,"* as it is known. As we sat, as we talked, I avoided the question(s) as to why I needed to head-on out Keng Tung way. Awh, the nothing-ness of life and conversation in Burma.

*   *   *

The heat of the dust/dirt on the road—though it was partially paved, pounded on my soul. The buses, generally white by nature, came went. Hundreds, no thousands of people, on and off of them. Carrying, crops in baskets, some over their shoulder, some placed upon their head. Some were orange clad Buddhist monks.

No place left to be. The sound, the vibration, the intensity of the depth of the people's wandering eyes; the dirt, the living, the religion. What does it?

What does life, all add up to? What does it all mean anyway?

My bus came. Got the old hand shake from uncle. I piled on. Others piled on. Thousands of others. ...Million of others. I was (obviously) the only white boy in transit.

They came in their droves; golden dark skinned. They carried their packages of purpose. What a pretense.

They, like I, chose to pretend that it all meant more than nothing. That it all added up to something/anything at-all. They squeezed next to me on the seat where I sat.

With no place left to run, they stood. Some of them planted themselves upon the floor.

Finally, we motored on. Each of us into our own individual destiny. But, for this moment, our paths crossed—meaning nothing, adding to little, just a passing glance in the trance of this life.

We motored on, out of town. The city scene soon faded to the natural vegetation and the occasion farm of the countryside.

Periodically, people would get off. Most jumped, while the bus was still in motion. Some, however, brought it to a full-on stop; as they had things to retrieve from atop.

Others would get on. They flagged the driver dude down. Mostly, it was pure, full-on claustrophobia. The freedom, the air, the blue sky was outside. It was not inside. No, it was not here.

The people, the power, the passion, and oh yes, the staring. I guess I was a curious site.

Fuck, this was going to be a long ride...

*　　*　　*

The distance, measured in miles, was probably only about two hundred and fifty. But, the roads of Burma, not being of the modern highway breed, we bounced more than a bit.

Finally, though I knew that I would lose my seat, I couldn't take it anymore. The stench of the people that haven't had a bath since who known when and haven't washed their clothing in probably forever. The smell of the crops they had in their bags... The clogged and clouded breathing air... I was about to explode.

Me, I went for the bail. I just couldn't take the inside anymore.

I grabbed my small brown leather bag. A little piece that I had picked up at a department store in Bangkok—solely for the purpose of this journey. It, and I, we made it for the back.

I stepped over a few dozen people on my way. Me, I hit the back door. Reached it, while the bus motored on. I slipped the handles of the bag down around my arm a bit. I swung out, grabbed the ladder, and I climbed up on top.

There were crops, baggage, a local or three sitting topside. I moved some of the stuff around; made myself a seat. Zipped open my bag. Grabbed my safari style hat. You know the kind, like Aussies wear into battle, with like one side snapped up. Did it, you know, to protect myself from the sun. I placed it upon my head.

There I was, in all of my glory; motoring East—the wind blowing through my long blonde hair. Had the bad sky-piece up top side. My brown baggy pants, on my *bod.* A blue long-sleeved outback shirt covering my form. A travel vest, khaki. And the dreams, they were caressing my mind. They just seemed oh so fucking haveable.

*   *   *

Here it was, only the fourth day. Goddamn, only the fourth day of the session up north. Sixth day, since I had entered the country. There had been a whole lot of living done in only a few days. Lived when the illusions are oh so close at hand out here *on the hard road.*

*   *   *

I pulled on into the town, it was coming up fast on sunset. All the locals knew where they were. But me, being no-go in the department of Burmese, had to keep asking, *"Keng Tung?" "Keng Tung?"* at every town we pulled on through.

I mean like, two hundred or so miles do go awfully slow on a bus, on the roads of Burma.

I was told, *"Yes,"* with a smiling nod. I must say, the people of are a nice breed.

I piled on down from the ride. Climbed down the ladder. I stood there, lost in realms of no return. Not really knowing where I was or how to get there.

The town... Well, the same as other stops in Burma. Old and wooden; filled with the dreams that die hard in a land lost under the shadow of the Buddha. There were a few businesses. Basically, Burmese style—semi outdoor establishments.

The eyes of the people, they were upon me. Yeah, I guess, like I was a bit of a rare creature in this neck of the woods. Not many of us white boys had rolled on through town for a while.

And no, no one had stopped me from riding the bus. The bus to Keng Tung. And no, there was no local government official ready to pounce; attempting to hinder my progression on to the hinterlands where all the illusion and all of the pain dwell.

I was riding solo: cool and slow. There were no obstacles in my way.

* * *

It was getting dark. I looked at the scene around me. That feeling of, *"Oh God, what have I gotten myself into,"* came over me. The signs, they were not in English, as they were at some of the non-restricted lo-cals in other sections of Burma. They were in Burmese—a written language that is more than geometrically beautiful. But fuck if I could figure any of it out.

Some signs were in Chinese. But, that too, is a written language that more-or-less escapes me; except for the most simple of memorized characters—even though I can speak a few dialects of it.

Me, I walked. What else could I do?

Now, I had this address written down, you know. But it was in English, so I couldn't really be directed.

The address pointed to a teashop on Airport Road. But, where the fuck was that. And, I was sure that the word airport must be said differently in Burmese.

I knew I had to get a crib. I looked for hotel or guesthouse sign. But, saw none.

Like hey, you either control the world or it controls you. And I'll be goddamned if I was going to let this place control me. I mean like in life, things happen to all of us: good, bad, whatever. You can either let them control you or you make the best out of them—make them an adventure; an experience. From this, then you will have won.

I mean like hey, this is reality; love it or leave it, you know.

*   *   *

I strutted on. I came upon this two-story wooden building. Looked like as good a shot as any for a crib zone. I went on in.

No one at the desk, so, *"Hello, hello."* A dude comes out, with a more than surprised look upon his mug.

"Is this a hotel?"

Amazements of all amazements, he did speak just a bit of English. Obviously, the missionaries/mercenaries had gotten to him, I guessed. And yeah, I could shack up there. He took me upstairs, showed me my room.

It was a cool little chamber. Wood walls. Had a bunk nailed into said wood walls. A window with no glass and a mosquito net, hanging from the ceiling, to be strategically extended and placed around the bed and the bod, in the hours of the evening.

Threw my bag down. Sat for a minute. Jotted in my journal. But, I quickly realized, I remembered that there was a reason that I had come to this town; one reason only.

I went back down the stairs, asked the homeboy for the direction to Airport Road. He gave them to me. It was a small town; not too hard to find.

I walked down the street in the relative coming cool of the evening air. There was still movement; everyone had not drifted off to the never-never-land of dreamland sleep. No, not as of yet.

A few people walked—some my way, some other ways. A bicycle here or there. An occasional, *"Hello,"* came my direction from the young children who hid in the sanctuary of their homes. Yes, the missionaries had gotten this far, as well.

Mostly, there were a lot of stares of disbelief. Some even came to their porch or to the outside of their nestled homes just to check the vibes of this foreigner walking on down their street.

I was not sure if I felt way-on fully cool for being such a sight or dismayed at the amount of geared-up psychic energy that was being pushed my direction. But, no longer was there any choice. I had to find her. Though, in truth, I was a bit uneasy. The thought to split in the direction of Rangoon, then just head on to Dacca, as I had originally planned, did come to mind. Or, maybe go back to Bangkok, where I knew all the chicks would just lie to me as they always did. *"I love you!" You're my first!"* Whatever…

But, with knowing every word spoken is a lie, there is a certain sublime truth present. As there was/is never anyone or anything to believe; it sets you free to just live the enlightenment of the night.

But, here I was; hooked—hook, line, and sinker. Lost in the discomfort of the not knowing what to expect—not knowing what I would find. Yet, I danced on.

I made it to Airport Road with little incident. I walked down the now darkened street, studying the structures, trying to determine which may hold my desired dream. I let the vibes; her vibes, Kyi Hlaing's vibes, pull me, guide to where she obviously must lay in wait of my touch, as I of hers.

I came upon a building; wooden like most of those before in the lost realms of Burma. The street was dark, but there was talk coming from the inside. A teahouse? Maybe?

I issued my way towards a door, behind a porch, which held wooden tables. I, following the light, walked forward.

I stepped upon the porch. I was met by a young *Lil' Soul Cous,* maybe three or four years of age. He was all smiles: friendly like most of the faces one meets in Burma. I asked him if this was the teashop. He just turned, ran to where the light was brighter.

Out comes this older man: gray, a bit of a beer gut, hanging loose. Kinda looked at me funny,

"Lapay," He asks.

(Burmese for tea).

"No, Kyi Hlaing."

Now, he really looked at me funny. If looks could kill, you know…

I figured that I had arrived at the right place.
He turned. He vanished. I stood there, alone.

*   *   *

waves of wonder

they poor upon us
slowly they caress our soul
when there is no way to go home
and the wish
is the command
desire is the god
as we stare
into the lost abyss
of the alone

*　　*　　*

I always have been one of those people to want to make the perfect entrance. You know, like to plan the whole approach. Just the right thing to say/just the right thing to do. Or, like when a babe comes over to my abode of love: the music, the setting, the light, it has to be just right.

So, I stood there on the porch in a pose. Like something from an old black and white movie. I stood there leaning against a wooden brace that held the roof up and over he patio. I stood there staring off into the city night, *cool'n,* like I just didn't care.

I heard the approaching footstep. But, I was too cool to turn and to see who was a-coming.

"Samuel?" I turned and saw a more surprised, then a welcoming face, staring directly into mine. Had I done the right thing?

It was the basic, *"Hellos;"* an occasional smile, but I could tell/feel something wasn't straight. We conversed in the basic level-one of English that she had and she invited me to sit upon one of the wooden benches, skirting one of the wooden tables, upon the wooden porch.

I guessed it was mama who came out to check my form. A peering eye, through a peering door, from the light into the darkness, gawked at me.

"I just wanted to see you again."
"How can you come here to a restricted zone?"
"I just came. Nobody stopped me."

Not to bore you here, but the *convo* went on as above. Mostly, I was just all about my cool and my charm. Predominantly, she was removed, stunned, sullen, and hidden.

I excused myself, thinking, *"Well, fuck me, this had sure added up to nothing; like the story of my life."*

I told her that I had a room at this guesthouse and that I was tried, so, *"See ya."*

I walked away, down the darkened street, as the bugs buzzed and amassed themselves around any type of artificial light that may be found. Me, I knew that I would never see her again.

I walked up the wooden stairs to my wooden room, climbed under the mosquito net. I lay there and listened to the perpetual music that was playing full-volume over some distant loud speaker. A calling, a message, telling all nighttime, wayward distant travelers, the pathway to this city on the fringes of nowhere. Yes, it was too loud.

And me, being the kind of guy that can't sleep to the vibrations of artificial noise. I lay there. I stared into the night; into the net, and wondered as I always do, *"Why do I do such stupid things?"*

Part V

I had gotten some sleep; not much. It was the early morning hours and there were some other constituents of the said establishment stomping, and I do mean stomping down the hall. It seems to me that people who walk heavy, are very insecure, as they are subliminally attempting to draw attention to themselves.

Well anyway, I was up. I was out of the sack jack. Had to go hit the head. Didn't really know where it was, but I played it cool, just chilled around: looking, checking; until it was found. It was an outhouse, out back, outside, of course.

There were two; one was occupied and one was not. I went in and met a whole shit load of flies. *"Shit load,"* get it? I mean their numbers were massive.

Now, in actuality, I had to pinch a loaf, but there was no way in the fucking world that I was going to squat down over one of those Asian style, no seat, just a hole in the ground, toilets, and let flies make a b-line for my asshole. So, I settled for just hanging one. Have to hold the other until better accommodations could be found.

Back up in my room, I got my bag together and was basically in the mode of bail. I mean like what was the purpose of hanging tight, you know? Fuck the love sick. Fuck the desire. I was going solo mobile. Figured I could go and hit the bus stop and pick up a ride for either Mandalay or preferably Rangoon, where there was still a chance that I may make by seven-day visa period of proper exit.

Yes, that was it. I could go back to Bangkok. Fuck the poverty of Dacca, my originally planned destination. Bangkok, yeah, where every dream is so fucking haveable.

Just as I was about to leave the room and pay up my bill, there was a knock on my door. I went to it and it was the dude who ran the place. In his best English possible, he laid down the fact that there was someone downstairs to see me. My first thought was, *"Fuck, the government has found me out. Better make for the backdoor and slide it on out-a-there."* But then, I thought, if they did catch me, that was okay, for I would just tell them that I did not know that it was restricted and I would bail onto Rangoon. Hell, maybe they'd give me a free ride. And maybe, just maybe, they even could get me on a flight instead of a bus. Yeah!

As I went down the stairs though, somehow the whole sensation changed—like a vibe, a feeling, came over me, that it was not the cop'ers. He pointed, and there, out on the porch, stood a woman. Yes, standing almost as posed and as cool as I had been the night before. There she stood staring into the daylight. I mean like, it was one of those poses that you see in the movies; with the sun reflecting in her hair and all. Yes, it was her, Kyi Hlaing.

It was all fully like a fear too real. Like, where I go from here? Like, when all that you wanted is placed in the palm of your hand…

I mean, I almost had to do the turn and slice my way on out-a-there. But, just as I was turning to bail, *"Samuel…"*

*   *   *

Just now, I glanced/stared into a photo. A photo from Burma that I took. It just caught my eye.

It hangs on my wall. My wall, over there. A photo of an illuminated golden Buddha.

I turned. I saw it here in L.A. Saw it, as these pages take their form.

Behind me there is a movement, I hear a noise. My new and currently main L.A. babe. She is crashed-out over there in my bed. I hear her sleeping movement(s).

Yeah, she is Asian too; on the grow up in Orange County, California, side of the coin.

I hear her. But, the image of the photographed Buddha, the thought of Burma, takes hold of my mind.

I caught sight of that photograph. It hit an emotion. An emotion of sadness. Sadness, buried deep inside of me.

But, people like me, we don't feel. Don't you know?

People like me, we have experienced just too much experience—lived just one to many. No, we don't feel. No, not any longer.

But goddamn, sometimes when you look back, you can't help but fucking wonder how things all got so fucked up and how the things that should have been, never could have been.

Well, I guess life is all perfect, you know— each event/each happening... Perfect in an imperfect world. Perfect in the metaphysical sense of the definition. Perfect, but it doesn't always feel that way.

Again, here we find another glimpse into the illusion of the no illusion—words that promise reality/enlightenment/a promise/a path/a way out/a way in/a method to justify the lies/a means to preach to the masses/a method of justification for an illusion that is this place we call life. An illusion with no real illusion. All bullshit by any other diction.

And, I wish I knew then, what I know now—that love means nothing. And no, it can never last. No, not really. Not in the world I live in anyway. Not in this altered reality that is call, *"My lifetime."*

And damn, I wish I had a life instruction manual to see what was coming around that next bend. The next bend that I will relive on these next few pages for you.

*   *   *

We sat down, on the wooden patio, in the warm Burman sun. She wore a blue wrap around dress—different from the original one; day of meeting and all, a tan shirt, and her skin seemed to melt into the color of the unpaved road which lay to her side.

Yes, we sat down, her and I. It was like a fucking movie. She smiled, I smiled, and it didn't mean a goddamned thing. We spoke of all of the basics of the nonsense that people tend to do. Me, I wanted more…

I am one of those one hundred percent full-on people. I mean like why wait; either do it or do not do it. Don't fuck around; don't waste time.

The Buddha, he was wrong. There is no such thing as the middle path. Life is either yes, or life it is no. Did he live the middle path; I don't think so; no.

Some people they can't hang with that—the undefined/the middle. They want to play the games. They want to dance. To me that is all like doing business. Yeah, love is like doing business. You give them what they want: be it beauty, money, inspiration, sex, whatever, and they will love you. But, you turn that bad shit off and you are history. Don't let anyone tell you that it is any different. I mean like, *"Oh, honey, I love you." "Oh, honey, I love you, too." "Honey, I don't love you anymore." "Well then, fuck you, I don't love you either, honey."*

It was like when I was a kid and a Boy Scout. Yeah me, I was a Boy Scout. Can you believe it? *Troop 121, Hollywood, California.* In fact, I got promoted up to the position of Senior Patrol Leader after some time in the ranks.

Well me, I used to get all of the other dudes high when we would go backpacking in the mountains and stuff. I was a delinquent way back then. But, that's not the story.

The story is: We were waiting to enter into the building where we had our Tuesday night meetings, this one evening—some of the other dudes and me. This old lady came by with way too many groceries, purchased from the local store, a few blocks down the street. She asked if we would help her carry her burden. I don't know, we probably threw some *negatory* comments her direction; and it was no-go—being Boy Scout delinquents and all. One dude thought, he went for the trip; being the nice Jewish boy that he was. He came back maybe ten minutes later, with a twenty spot in his hand. I mean damn, nothing is free, not even helping old ladies. Fuck, I thought even then, if I was going to do it there was no way I would have accepted any change for my actions.

She is probably dead now. Just like we all will be someday. And what will it all mean then? The same as this recorded story. I guess nothing.

So, Kyi Hlaing told me of her family, her town and/or all of her basic sitch-e-ations. You know, how they never see foreigners here. How her family completely freaked when I showed up. How it isn't proper protocol for a dude to show up unannounced at the door of a girl he is courting; so on and etcetera.

It meant nothing to me. I came for love. I wanted it all!

"Oh, don't leave today. I want to show you around," came the statement.

Well, never give a gambler, like myself, a player's hand.

The day was young. I was young. Well, a few years younger than I am at this point in time. Young, yet I had nothing left to lose.

Me, I went and threw the owner of the guesthouse a few *kyat* notes to hold over my room for the interim. I mean, you never know where destiny will take you...

We, Kyi Hlaing and I, walked down the street, as more than a few eyes caught hold of yours truly. A few kids came up a-laughing. *"Fuck off,"* I haven't got time for this bullshit. I mean like my play is in motion.

You know, it is kind of funny; sometimes out there on the hard road. I mean like you want to be nice and cool and all, for it is the turf of others, and you have to like smile all the time. But, sometimes that fake smile shit just gets old and you just don't want to do it anymore.

But, the situation, her and I, it was all kinda like; where do you go from here? We walked around; zero in a zero world. I had seen this place/this space before: poverty, pain, Buddhism, all that bullshit. Yeah sure, it may have actually been a different town, a separate continent, but they are all the same. All the same like this babe. I should have realized it then...

We pulled into this little lay-low truck stop, of a *"Locals Only,"* hang out; grabbed up a cup of the tea and began to rap.

"My parents are very upset that a foreigner has come to visit me."
"Why?"
"They think that all of the town's people will look down on me."
"Why?"
"Well, because I was away, and most of these small minded people here believe that if a woman goes off to college she is a bad girl."
"Well, that's stupid."
"Yes, to you and I. But to them..."
"So I guess that it is better if I leave."

Gotta admit here, I don't know if it was ego, love, actually caring about another human being, or whatever, but there was a wee bit of a dropping feeling in my heart as all of this *convo* was being laid down.

"No, no, no, I don't want you to leave. I just want you to understand what is going on. But, I don't care what they think."

With that and with this, well it was AOK; chill factor zero with me. So, we ordered up some grub. Ate what we ate. Did what we did. And, were back *mobil'n* down the street.

It was getting to be afternoon by this point, and Mar Son had to hit on over and lay her college educated helping hands in the directions of her pappy's teashop. So, I walked her. We pulled up in front,

"Mommy."

Out comes a-cruising the little homeboy, of a few-year-old, who gave me the peer the evening last. *"Mommy!"* Well, fuck me.

They did the basic hugs and/or etcetera. And he, the soul *cous,* gave me the smiles and the stares that I had come to expect in this region.

Her eyes were full of embarrassment. Or maybe it was just the *"Oh no's... He, the love stud of my life, has found out."* I don't know?

I had to ask,

"Is that's your son?"
"Oh yes, isn't he beautiful?"

Right then. Before I could answer. Out comes pop, giving me the *negatory* stare.

"I have to go to work now. See you soon."

Me, I walk off into the sunset. Thinking, *"What the fuck did all of this mean?"* I mean, was she like latched up or what? Did she have a home daddy crib side? Or, was it like her old man, who put the bone into action and dorked her up; was he on the bail? Or, was he just hiding in the shadows?

I mean like, all of these kind of thoughts go through a dude's head, you know, when the *sitch,* is just not clear.

In any case, I strutted my bad stuff back to the five stars of the local circuit guesthouse hotel in the sky. Yeah right. I hit my room. Zoned out for a nap; a release. But, it was way too fucking hot. I can't sleep when it's hot.

You know, it is like, have you ever... I mean like has your mind ever woken up and your body lay there still asleep? And then, you have to try to move something, shake something; your foot or whatever, to try to pull yourself out of the hell of immobility; with your mind awake but your body still asleep? I don't know... That only seems to happen to me in the heat.

Once I had this friend and his mother was this full-on Latin home-girl of a believer in the Catholic faith. I mean like, I was maybe like twelve years old back then and she gives me the rap down that this had happened to her. She told me it was the devil trying to take possession of her soul. But, with her body immobile, her mind awake, she prayed. She prayed to god and she was saved.

Yeah whatever, bitch. I mean, *"Come on,"* how much bullshit is whipped up in the direction of the old devil. The devil, man's excuse for either not understanding something or not having the ability to take control over one's own body and desires. *Lay it to rest...*

So anyway, I lay there; no sleep. So me, I got up; went and hit the chow wagon, down the street. Some dude wanted to rap in his bad broken English. I wasn't in the mood.

Pop the chow, I went back to the crib and sacked out.

In all of the confusion I spent another night with the plans of bail come sun up.

Part VI

Come the morning; amazingly, I was still asleep. I'd slept through all of the bullshit blasted music than rang in my ears through the night, announcing the location of the town where I lay my head to the meaningless wayward travelers. I must have been very tired. But, there came to me a knock upon my door.

Jumping up, I had to untangle myself from the mosquito net. I went, opened my door and it was soul boy proprietor from the downstairs. I had a visitor. I wondered who that could be???

*   *   *

The air breathes hot in Southeast Asia. The air pounds on your soul. The wind is hot. The days are hot. The nights are hot. Maybe that it is why Buddhism is so full-on, you know. It promises, escape.

Have you ever really wanted to escape a situation? Have you ever really wanted to get out, but you did not know where to run or how to run or even sure if you could run?

It was like when I was a child. The memory came to mind. I remembered... There was this beauty parlor that I went to with my Grandmother; maybe twice, maybe three times. I just don't know... But, she went there to get her gray hair dyed blue; you know the deal.

Now, as you may know from some of my other books, or maybe you even know me, but I spent my early years down on the wrong side of the tracks in L.A. Southcentral is the name that has most recently been attached to the region. So, I guess we will go with that. In any case, it was the ghetto. I was literally the only white kid in my grammar school. But, like the territorial animal that all people are, I had my stomping grounds. And though, the region was full-on black, in cultural origin and racial terms; me, being a white boy, (white paddy or honky as I was constantly called), I had my turf staked. I knew where I could walk, with more-or-less safety, and the etcetera.

Now, I was maybe six, maybe seven, when I used to hit the beauty parlor with my grandmother. We would drive on down and into the region where it was located.

It was South—down farther South; such as South goes in the ghettos of L.A. I would see this world: the dilapidations of the surroundings, the poverty, the lack of life in the lifeless. I would see it and I would feel the fear. I knew, in this region, there was no longer any safety.

Walking from the car, her 1964 Chevy Nova, parked in front of the beauty shop on the street, I could taste it—the fear.

It was not just me. Everyone around me feed on it/lived off of it.

Inside the shop, I would stare out of the window as my grandmother would get her hair done. I would observe. I can still see it all, in my mind's eye; a white house, across the street. It was like the backside of this white house. I could see the alley that ran down and divide the white house from a green house. I could see the backs, the sides. I could see, breathe in the poverty. There were ancient fences around these house(s); promising untrue safety. Old fences. Broken fences. Chain link fences. There were trashcans, in the unpaved dirty alley. Overfilled, the trash piled out of them. Them, the metal trashcans.

I never saw any people in those houses. But, I know that people must have lived there. Living, as the paint chipped off of the walls of the outside. Living, as cockroaches and rodents ate their souls/had their fills, on the inside.

I lived, experienced, and breathed the fear of that world. Observed, from the safety of the beauty shop owned and operated by an old white lady.

The old white women, (like my grandmother), would make their way to, and lock themselves inside, the protection of the metal-head buckets; big, green, hair-heating machines. All the things that a white woman, with bluing hair needed, in an Afro world.

The lady. The beautician. She lived upstairs. Upstairs in a decaying brick building. Decaying, she had no place left to run, and no desire left to get there. She had been located in this place, in this region, long before it went to hell in a handbag— many-many years ago.

Desire, I hold that key, that burden.

I never had the chance to tell my Grandmother, *"Good bye."* Never had the chance to tell her that she was, *"Way cool," "Way nice,"* to me. Didn't see her, the last ten, last fifteen years of her life. But that's another story...

And why do I tell you all of this? Why, you ask?

The fear, the burden of a white boy in a black world, where they were far more prejudice than I ever was. The fear of the decaying/displaying streets. It was the same here/now. This time in Burma.

I don't know why it came, the instinct/the understanding. But, it did come. Damned if I didn't know something was a-coming down. Something big/something bad was about to go down.

*   *   *

I walked down the hallway; I sweated. I walked down the stairs; I hyperventilated. I stepped out into the glow of light, which looked like an cosmic aura frame around my new love. It was way fucking scary. Goddamn, I wanted to run in any direction but into her arms.

I controlled the fear, though. I repressed in deep inside me. Hid it, like I did all the years of my youth. Isn't that it what, *"A real man,"* is supposed to do?

I walked outside, into the heat, that left me no room to run, no room to breathe. I knew/understood that I was dancing into the devil's game, but I knew I was paying a loser's hand.

But, like a man, I walked on…

"Hey, what's up?"
"Good morning. Did you sleep well?"
"Yeah. Like, AOK, babe…"

It was as if there was this great wall in front in me and I did not know any way of climbing over it. Because of and as such, I walked straight into it—smashing the hell out of my face.

She took me by the hand; literally. She walked us down from the porch. She escorted me down the street.

Now, let me just give you a little preface here…

As previously stated, this chick did not speak English too well. So, I am going to be doing a little translating here; for her. If you catch my drift. I mean like, you kind had to be there to even begin to understand her. So, I won't put you through all of that.

"Samuel, I have a son."

Oh, surprise, surprise…

"Do you still like me?"
"Why wouldn't I?"
"Because I didn't tell you before. Are you mad at me?"

Yeah, that's right, you didn't, ho… I mean like I place my butt in gear and jam all the way over here, to the far side of nowhere, going through who knows what, maybe getting my butt tossed in the local can for you who I thought was worth the journey and oh, surprise, surprise, you have a little bundle of joy. You goddamned right I am mutha fucking pissed off.
I thought that. But, my smile, my words spoke something different.

"Oh, of course not. I am not mad at all."

Bitch…

"Oh, that's good. I thought that you might be upset."
"Where is your husband," I inquire.

A bit of sadness hits her old eyeballs, here, at this point.

"I do not have a husband."

At this point, some little kids run up to us as we walked down the dirt-paved path.

"Peace, peace. Hello. Money."

They have their hand out.
Hit the trail kid!
Naturally, I have a smile on my face. But, we keep walking.
We walk a bit farther, the kids still in tow.
Then, we come upon one of the millions, one of the many Buddhist Stupas, which grace the sight of this country. It is tall, white, a pinnacle, which points its way to the god(s), to enlightenment, to the Buddha, which resides in the sky. Me, I make prayer hands at it.
The kids laugh. They run off. They leave us alone.
The sky is the piercing blue color that only *Mata Burma* has the keys to present. The vegetation is to our sides; browning green.
We sit at the far side of the aforementioned temple. The dirty Southeast Asian white wall of the shrine supports our backs as we sit down on the ground and lean against it.

"Why don't you have a husband?"
"He was killed."
"Killed? By who?"
"Mercenaries."

Mercenaries/missionaries. Remember…

"How did that happen?"
"He was not such a good man, I must say."
"What do you mean?"
"He did not so good of things."
"Like what?"

Naturally, being the inquisitive soul dude that I am.

"Well, you Western people… Some of you like drugs; yes?"
"Yeah, I guess."

Me, paying it all Mr. Innocent and stuff.

"Well, he tried to help Western people buy drugs. There are these people in the mountains, they grow and make drugs. Everybody here, they know where this place is. Sometimes these people who grow drugs, they don't like the other people that grow drugs. So, they kill each another."

A tear or two, hits the scene here.

Well hell, let me paraphrase. I mean like fuck me, this is really not what I want to be hearing. I mean, I am just not one of those sensitive, everything is groovy, sort of self-actualized guys. I mean like, I just do not want to hear all of this bullshit about some other dude and see the tears that his memory brings on.

She continues…

"And so, one day, my husband tried to help these Western people buy drugs. They wanted a lot of drug. And so, he took them up there to the mountains, where you can buy much drugs. But, he not know that this one big drug man have a fight with another big drug man. When he go mountains, he buy drug with the Western man. When they are coming back, they all got killed. (tear, tear). So, before you, I always hate Western man."

Post a tear of three,

"You not like that kind of Western man. I know..."

If only she knew...

With this, she leans her head over and lays it on my shoulder. Me, being Mr. Sensitive, (at least in the sense of pretend), I put my arm around her. Soon, there is a kiss planted upon my cheek. I turn to look from *wenst* it came. She slaps another one right there upon my lip line.

Fuck me, man! My destiny was sealed.

From there, (this day I describe to you), the time, it got lost. Lost into all of the stupid oblivion that infatuation has to offer.

I won't bore you with the next few days that came to pass. Mostly, it was just time lost to never-never-land of *gaga* love. She would come morning-side each day. The dude would wake me up. Well, in truth and in actually, I came to wake up early and be lying there in bed awaiting his footsteps and the knock upon my door. The days were spent in holding hands, when and where none of the locals could see us, of course. And, an occasional kiss here and there. Then, she would be off at work. To work at her daddy's tea shop. And me, I would be staring off into the space of Keng Tung, wondering what the fuck to do.

*   *   *

I would show up on her doorstep, in the evening hours, post having a day of walking, observation, and mostly waiting for the evening to come around when she would have some time again. Yeah, that was time; a time ago. Then, we would dance out to the city streets; dirt streets, and we would walk down them. I would be laid that occasional light lover's kiss. Me, naturally; I wanted more/I wondered when more would come.

I remember watching, *The Love Boat* on T.V. God, it must have been more than ten years ago.

I used to live in this apartment out in L.A.'s, *The Valley;* back when I was an undergraduate. The apartment was relatively close to my university and all…

In it, I had this bad little black and white T.V. that my father had given me for my tenth birthday. In fact, it was the last present that he ever gave me before he died. It used to sit on the floor next to the foam pad upon which I slept. Sometimes, I would lay on my foam pad and watch early morning re-run T.V on it.

I remember, *The Love Boat,* was on. It was this story about this guy who latched up with this chick on the boat, and, as it turns out, she was knocked-up with some other dude's spawn. The guy wanted her to get an abortion but she was no-go in that *departmento*. So, it was this up and down and back and forth *thAng.* Initially, he dumped her. Then, he finally said that it was just his male ego, etcetera, etcetera, etcetera. In the end, he took the *ho* back.

Now personally, I would have handed her the, *"You're history,"* statement, myself. Like, *Homey, don't play that.* I mean, a real dude, a dude's dude, doesn't want to forever be reminded of who had been in his bitch's hanger of love. But damn, here I was, locked up in a similar sit-e-ation, with this chick. But, that love pounded in my heart, though I admittedly wondered why. It bothered me everyday, the question, *"Why?"* Then I would be with Kyi Hlaing and it/the thoughts/the questions would all go away.

Anyway...

Love! Damn, I don't know... Why does it happen? Even when you do not wish, desire that it would/should occur?

*   *   *

But anyway... Excuse my indulgence. Onto the rest of the story, or at least to the point.

I just do not believe that relationships can last. It is like, they are there, and then they are history—one way or the other.

I mean like, I will be goddamned if we aren't all going to die someday... Or, something is going to happen. Or, someone is going to find someone else. Or, whatever....

So me, I am one of those dudes that just sabotages a relationship long before it ever has the opportunity to fully blossom. Kept myself safe, you know.

Needless to say, by this point; I don't know, what was it, maybe six days into the local terrain of,

Love Connection. So me, I had to the word *"Bail,"* written all over me.

*   *   *

It was night. We/her, Kyi Hlaing, and I; well, we sat at her father's teashop. We sat across the table from one another, in the warm heat of the pounding night. Moths, bugs, whatevers; they formed their images; illustrating that lack of perfection, at least in my perception, of God's evolutionary environment. I hate bugs! They encircled the light which hung from the ceiling of the room.

We moved outside. We sat outside. A bug or thirty bothered me there, as well.

We sat on the wooden table and chairs. She sat across from me. Or I, across from her. Depending on your point of view. She looked at me. It was a piercing, almost violent look, that went straight to the heart of my soul.

"Nothing else matters, Samuel. Whatever has happened before means nothing to me. No one has ever touched my heart like you. I love you. And, I will love you forever."

Well, fuck me! Her words ripped the, *"Bail,"* from my mind.

Place the plastic passion, of all of those innate DESIRE movies, upon the movie screen. I mean like, I really believed her. I fell headlong into the inescapable trap.

I mean fuck, she didn't have, *"Green card,"* written in her eyes. She didn't have, *"$,"* written in her eyes. No, not like all the other Southeast Asian bitches. She wanted nothing; only me.

Like, a fool, I believed. I bought the ticket.

After a gently kiss on my lips, and the word of, *"Forever,"* coming from them, I walked home; back to my hotel, guesthouse like crib, with all the flutters of a new born adolescent. Filled with all the thoughts that the stuff on T.V., that I had doubted, well, maybe it could be for real. Love could be perfect. It could last forever. Yeah me, I believed...

I lay in bed that night, covered with mosquito netting, of course; damn, if it wasn't hard to sleep. Not from the noise outside but from the noise inside—my brain rumbled. Like, what was I going to do now? Now, that I had what I thought I had always dreamed of but had always run from. I mean like, here I am in a country; a country that I was supposed to have left: four, five, six, whatever, days the previous. There, and in love. Now, I was going to have to try the bail with a babe in tow. How, was I going to explain this/that one?

This was not going to be easy. No, not the way this government is run.

Finally, I chilled to a sufficient level. I lay out. I slept. A new day was coming, and there was much on the horizon. Too much, in fact. I wish someone would have let me know, what was coming next.

Part VII

I was waiting this morning as she walked up—waiting on the porch outside of my guesthouse. The proprietor did not have to come a-knocking. I had my cool sky piece on, topside, to protect my face from the rays. You know the one. The Aussie style hat. I wore my brown baggy pants, a kaki shirt, my once loved *Puma Power Cat* tennis shoes. We, her and I, were headed, as an Aussie would say, for a *walk-a-bout*.

Yes, she my love, Kyi Hlaing, had the day off. Something that is almost impossible in a family owned business, in a country like Burma, and all. Well, and however, she got it—the day off that is. How? I do not know. But, she got it.

There was this place which she wanted to take me to. I was like way up for the ride. I mean like, pacing the same streets on the far side of the backside, like I/like we had been doing for several days now, had gotten a bit old.

She strutted up in all her elegant beauty; wearing a light olive-green top, a blue wrap around skirt *thAng*, and thongs. Of course, she had her parasol.

It/she was quite a stunning picture as she proceeded along the dirt road, paved by the unkempt and the unclean. But, anyway…

We hit over the edge of town and picked up this little pickup truck of a covered in the back, public transportation type of *thAng*. You know, like a bench down each side of the bed of this blue pickup truck and a green canvas top covering the back.

We zoned and bailed on for points unknown. Down the dusty road we moved.

Kyi Hlaing and I sat side-by-side, occasionally turning to stare into one another's eyes *'de love* and reaffirm the promise of passion; the guarantee of forever. Mostly though, I would stare out into the passing abyss of the green verging on brown vegetation; semi tall trees, that attempted to, but could not reach the sky.

There were occasional people who would ride with us. Mostly, their eyes would fall to me; with the occasional wonder of why a local woman, such as Kyi Hlaing, would be with me. Words would be spoken among themselves, but never to us. Then, we were left alone, out there on the extremities of nowhere. Alone, for miles unspoken. We spoke no words. Nothing to say. Nothing needed to have been said; as the road passed, as the moments passed, as our lives ticked. Left only to these few written words that have so little meaning. Little meaning, like this day I live today; empty, oblivious; seeking to be something more than nothing. Seeking to be somewhere else/doing something else. I search. I cry out. I try to find an answer. But, zero is all that is left.

I remember that moment, the space in time when I first felt that zero. I experienced it as we rode down the dirt road that day. I wanted… I had dreamed, fantasized, that it would mean something more. But, like today; plans they are meaningless. Plans, they always seem to equal nothing.

I passed a glance over to her, my woman, my love of the time. I wanted, I desired, I screamed, I almost cried for it to mean more. But, this ride, this life; like days, like today, it meant nothing. I searched but there was no meaning to find.

*　　*　　*

Eventually, we came to our stopping point. Kyi Hlaing pounded on the rear window of the truck. Our chauffeur stopped. With smiles all around, we climbed out of the back.

The air breathed warm that day. The sky was intense blue. The ground was dry. Its color, almost; yeah, almost red. I saw what appeared to be a palm tree, several of them, in fact, intermixed with palmly vegetation. Yeah, this was Southeast Asia.

The truck drove off. We walked off. I could not help but wonder what was going to be our way back to the realms of semi-civilization, once our journey of the day had been completed. I wondered. But, I was way too *macho* to ask. We walked on...

It was just past the grove of those palm type trees that I witnessed upon our stop. Never would I have known that it was there. But, we passed through them, the palm type trees, and there was a river. A river flowing muddy dark brown and green. She told me that we were to sit there, to wait there. For what, who could ever know?

She cleared a spot for me, one for her. Then, she lay down a handkerchief for herself to sit upon. I looked/I smiled/I guessed I was to sit unencumbered in the dirt.

But me, I remembered/thought, how once upon a time, in a brief stay, in a brief/meaningless place, I remembered when I was ten years old... Yeah, back visiting Middle America, I had sat down on the grass for a few, rap'n with some local acquaintances. Post our rap, I got up, went home, later to find my butt covered with red bumps. I was told it was this bug, *Chiggers*. They were/are blood sucking sons-of-bitches and you have to do all this shit to get rid of them. I remembered that. And, fuck if I was going to sit down and get some local *Mata Burma* bug crawling under my skin. Fuck that. I remained standing.

The pagan pale blue of the Burma sky embraced me. I remember it so clearly, like it etched itself into my soul. The clouds, white. They passed slowly across the sky; Eastward—heading to locations unknown. I stood there, in dried river mud, with the water of the river flowing in front of me, Kyi Hlaing, sitting to my side. The green, verging on brown, vegetation to my rear. And damn, if I didn't feel like a caged fucking house cat, knowing that there must be a world outside of myself, but not quite sure what it was, where it was, or how to get from here to there.

Probably twenty past our session of wait, time gets weird out there in the out-back, a boat came upon the rivers bend and I could see it gravitating in our direction. It was a long boat, not too dissimilar from those that cruise the Chao Praya in Bangkok. But somehow, it looked/felt different. Like, it was sent from some alien source, destined to drive me to the realms of Hell, where I must fight my way back to Heaven.

Kyi Hlaing suggested that I wave it over. Over it came. We boarded.

We sat on it, nearer to the front, than the three other locals that sat behind us. There was just enough room for her and I to sit next to each other, under the shade of the canopy, which was attached to the boat and suspended above our heads.

Kyi Hlaing explained where it was that we wanted to travel to the ship's captain. Post that, no further words were spoken; at least not to us.

Though I knew, the boat driver at the stern, guiding the boat, and/or the other locals, must have made some comment about this Anglo riding hand-in-hand with Kyi Hlaing, for she had become somewhat uncomfortable. Me, I could feel the pressure of their eyes burning a hole in the back of my skull. I wanted to turn around and kick their fucking asses. But instead, I chilled and just stared off into the space of Burma vegetation and the river that I suspect never ended, just flowing on-and-on-and-on into the nowhere realms of reality and stuff like that there.

The river flowed, the boat flowed, life flowed, and we flowed. Kyi Hlaing never removed her hand from mine on that hour plus boat ride we took. I came to believe it was a sign of love... Never removed her hand, even when the boat stopped two times to let off the previously aforementioned passengers. I was glad to see them leave.

It was so much freer when only Kyi Hlaing, the captain, and I were left on the boat. I don't really know why; maybe it was the vibes... But somehow, the whole river world became more alive. I felt it!

Does that sound weird? Maybe... But it was/is like: the river, nature; it all began to speak to me. And no, I was not duped up on any acid or anything like that. But, it was like, I just experienced the beauty of the perfection of this place. The green brown river. The massive almost tropical vegetation. The passive blue of the sky. I mean, it felt like I could live here/there forever, you know. Live there, while holding Kyi Hlaing's hand throughout eternity.

Live forever... Live forever there. But, nobody lives forever. Nobody lived there. Not anymore anyway. It sure didn't seem that way.

There was nobody. No structures. No nothing. Not since we had hit the village on the far side, where the last local homeboys had gotten out, you know. So, I didn't know what to expect.

Anyway, I won't go further into the geographic description as you have probably seen a similar scene in all of those fake Vietnam war pictures that are actually shot in Thailand or the Philippines. But, reminiscent of those places/those movies, as we crusaded down the river, I heard what seemed to be the distant sound of a gunshot; one, then two, then three. I looked at Kyi Hlaing, she didn't seem disturbed by it. So, I supposed I wasn't supposed to be disturbed by it.

I tried... I pretended... But, coming from the streets of L.A., where virtually everyone packs a piece, it was a sound I found hard to ignore.

Finally, Kyi Hlaing, broke her grip from mine. Thank god, my hand was full-on sweating. I mean like, fuck... She turned and told the driver to pull it in on over. He did. She slapped some change his direction and we were out-a-there.

Personally, I was seriously concerned how the fuck where we were going to get back. Kyi Hlaing, ignored the question, and we walked on—down *the yellow brick road* as it were. Well no, actually it was a dirt path.

I mean, here we were on a path to *no-wheres-ville Daddy-O*. I mean like, it sprang from nowhere and went on-to nowhere. Nowhere that I could see, anyway.

I was out here in the deep outback. I heard shots in the distance. I didn't speak the language. I had no idea where the fuck I was. Had no clue how to get back.

Think about it. How was I supposed to feel? Was I am lamb being led to the slaughter?

But, none-the-less, the journey continued.

We walked down it; the path that is. And, I don't know, call me a paranoid, but it all felt very-very strange. Like, you ever get that feeling? A feeling that you are someplace that you are just not supposed to be. I attempted to chill it back; hold it in wait. Be remaining calm, cool, collective, it was not so easy.

The vegetation rose around us; to my shoulders—reaching towards the sky: green/brown. I heard the birds singing in the trees; calling to something, crying to no one. It was hot as we walked. No source of refreshment. No place to run. Why, was I doing this?

Somehow though, as the walk continued, deeper-deeper-deeper... I don't know, maybe it was her holding my hand—never letting go; maybe it was her loving glances, maybe... But anyway, somehow this feeling of total suchness came over me. It etched away my innate disconcertment. In fact, a strange sense of contentment took hold. A feeling, I virtually never feel.

We walked on, as the birds sang, as the Southeast Asian, *Mata Burma,* heat pounded, as an occasional sound of what I thought to be gunfire came in from the distance. Kyi Hlaing, didn't flinch.

Finally, in all of its suchness, we arrived at this beautiful poppy flower field. I wondered would the scent of the opium poppies get me high? The field; green, with buds of light gleaming to the early afternoon sky.

There at the entrance rose this small grass hut. Green and brown, flaked to the top by the crystal blue sky. Like all sights around me, the colors moved to the sounds of the nature of Burma that seem to be something more—be, more than I ever could.

She smiled. We walked inside. Instantly, I felt sheltered, protected from the unknown realm(s) of the outside. Though there was no floor, *per se;* the ground had been brushed down and created into a bed by what appeared to be grass or maybe hay.

She knelt down; laid back. And, without a word, pulled me to the ground with her. My dick got hard.

Reaching around my head, she pulled my mouth to hers; we embraced. Then again and again. My tongue pushed its way through her teeth to find the previously inexperienced realms of possible bliss. Areas, which had never been known. And, like the kiss of a virgin goddess, it was the embrace of all that ever was. She allowed my tongue to caress hers. A feeling she had never experienced before. Goddamn, I was in love.

It was not like a kiss of an experienced woman who lied, claiming that she had never known a man. Fuck, I've met/known a lot of those. It was not like one of those embraces where the chick thinks she knows how to tongue, and then gives you a mouth full of teeth. Though of course, those all can be interesting in their own right. This was a kiss of the known unknown; love that had never been felt before.

She slipped free of her skirt. My hand found its way to her crotch. I massaged her semi-fresh patch of beaver hair. My finger found it soft, wet, wild.

Not in a mood to hurry the moment, I slowly removed her shirt. As her semi small golden breast shinned their glowing light upon me. My mouth, my body, my mind became enthralled in their seemingly perfect form.

She struggled to remove her shirt. I gave her a bit of a hand.

I kicked off my *Pumas,* unbuckled my belt, pulled down my zipper, and clumsily removed my pants.

There we were: safe, protected; dancing to the movements of a love that only sinners can feel. It was the moment of truth. My cock found its way home. I put it in very slowly.

With Kyi Hlaing, it wasn't a game. I didn't attempt to play any. I slide the dick slightly in. As I did, it was like the feeling of just going home. A home I had never known.

We made love for a long time. How long, I really do not know. But, it all came to the climax of its own perfection: Kyi Hlaing, me, that hut, the grass that we lay upon, and the seeming protection from the outside world.

She fell asleep when we were done. Tired, I suppose, from the trials and tribulations of her life and mind. And, though sex usually energized me; post its performance, I decided in all of the contentment of this moment that it was time to lay my cares to rest and sleep next to her. Sleep in her arms forever.

Have you ever known the feeling; ever thought the thought of like how dreams somehow, are in some way, better than life? I don't know... But, I began to dream as I slept in her arms. Dreamt I was in ancient India; wearing a white *dohti* and a *kurta.* Dreamt I was at the feet of Siddharth

Guatama, the Sakyamuni Buddha. I glanced up, to look at his face. But, just as I was about to see it, come eye-to-eye with him, the most holy of holy, I was rudely awoken from the dream. I was shaken, not stirred.

I woke to hear the sound of distant voices. Dazed, I wondered was I still dreaming. But no, I was not. I heard voices and they were getting closer.

I reached over to put on my clothing. Ready, as ready could be for action. In doing so, Kyi Hlaing awoke.

"People coming," I said. *"Maybe you better get dressed."*

As the voices came closer, I could make them out. They spoke in a strange Burmese/Thai dialect that I had not heard before. I did not understand what they had to say.

With our clothing on, I instinctively thought that it would be a-way better thing if we were not waiting for the on-comingness of these dudes, *Hut Central.* I took Kyi Hlaing by the hand and began to lead her to the door.

In that moment of motion, she stopped. Her hand was holding mine. She pulled me back. As she did, I witnessed her beautiful dark eyes staring into the depths of my soul. She smiled and pulled me close. She gave me a kiss. Once again, I was lost in all the pagan fields of love.

*   *   *

With the voices still approaching, I ended our embrace and headed for some less conspicuous cover; namely, the forest. Stepping within its bounds, all the paranoia of snakes, cobras, etcetera, and so on came to mind. But, I had to see what was a-coming down. So me, I peer over a tree.

There into the clearing walked these two dudes; fully dressed in camouflage attire and packing some serious *Kalashnikov*s.

Fuck, missionaries!

I decided it was time to exit stage left, if you know what I'm a-talking about.

I don't know, it's like one of those things you see on the T.V. shows; when some dude in tracking somebody else down. It's like, the people run and run, bringing all kinds of attention to themselves. I always thought, *"Why don't they just hide in a dark corner and then they will never be found."* Or, if they are tracked down, while hiding in the corner, then, at least, they will have the first-strike advantage as the dude who is doin' the trackin' will not expect them to be anticipating his oncoming approach. Then, *BAM,* you could smack 'em down hard.

I didn't listen to my own logic, however.

With a pretty good sense of direction, I was heading down for the river. I was pacin' it fast, somewhere to the side of the trail—bail central through the forest.

I remember thinking that I really didn't know what I would find, or where or how we would go, once we got to the water. But, that seemed like the best direction is which to head.

As we moved, I could feel the agitation in Kyi Hlaing. Perhaps it was fueled by me. But, let me tell you, I have spent too much time in Southeast Asia not to know when something isn't *kosher.*

We didn't speak. Our communication was telepathic. It was probably better that way. At least, so I thought. So I thought, as the trees and the shrubs smashed into our bodies/our faces as we bolted through the vegetation.

Just as we entered the river clearing... I mean like goddamn, I ran right into 'em; right upon to 'em. There they were, these three missionary guys. Immediately, they jumped up frightened at our surprised arrival.

Frightened, with their *Kalashnikov*s in hand.

*   *   *

Now FYI, I'm going to give you a translation here. A translation of what was said; what was translated by Kyi Hlaing to me, and what I just kind of figured out was being spoken. As mentioned, they spoke this weird dialect of Burmese/Thai. So, understanding was not on the front lines of reality.

I do want to mention, however, that; I got to tell you, it is pretty fucked up when dudes with some serious *gats* pointing at you are talkin' shit and you really/barely know what the fuck is being said. But, that being stated, I won't put your through all of the all-of. For, in fact and in truth, I really don't know how the fuck I could translate the non-translatable anyway. And, to keep the story more-or-less moving forward...

Anyway...

"Well, Hello. Who are you? What are you doing here? Who's the little lady?"

Says this one guy; standing maybe five foot nothing; wearing dirty camouflaged pants and a dirty khaki colored tee-shirt.

"My, my, where you from?"

Chimes in another one of the minus mutha fuckers, looking and wearing about the same.

"You from England?"

I looked them up and down with the hardest look I could muster. Thought I saw the hesitation in their eyes, I guess when your packing pieces the size of the ones which they were carrying, intimidation is not an easy thing to succumb to.

One of them walks towards Kyi Hlaing. I moved and stood in between him and her.

"No, I'm from America."

He smiles. He laughs. He asks.

"What are you doing up here, looking for dope?"
"Nope."
"Aren't you a little lost, then?"

They start to laugh. I knew this meant problems.

"We pretty much go where we want to go. Take what we want to take."

The one dude exclaims as he looks at Kyi Hlaing.

The ass-fuck then walks around me. He reached to caress Kyi Hlaing's hair. She pulls out of the way. I move. Look him straight in the eyes. He looks at his friends and then laughs.

"Doesn't look like you have much to say about what we do."

He says this as he lifts his rifle up slowly and partially.

I looked at him. I turned to Kyi Hlaing. I took her by the hand and began to walk from the scene. He grabs me by the shoulder. I pulled away.

"Where you going so soon? We're just getting to know each other."

Like all losers handed a piece of power, whether it's a gun, a job title, a bible, or being bigger than the other guy, they don't know what to do with it. That's what makes them the losers that they are; the losers that they always will be.

I looked at him, one more time.

"We're walking."

The asshole, sticks his rifle up to my chest and cocks it.

"No, I don't think you are."

In a flash, I shove the gun to the side. While holding onto the barrel, I roundhouse kick the ass-munch in the head. Due to my holding onto the gun; he still stands but is seriously shaken.

I pull the rifle away from him. I quickly spin it and hit him in the forehead with its butt.

The other two guys are jumping into action. I spin around behind myself, swinging the butt of the gun. I hit this other dude in the side of the head. He goes down hard.

The third dude cocks his gun. I do a stepping front kick and catch him under the jaw. His head snaps back. His gun goes off into the sky.

The three guys reasonably deuced, I toss the rifle on the ground, grab Kyi Hlaing, and run for the jungle—*run through the jungle.*

*   *   *

Time spins in these moments of intensity. We were running to god knows where. But, I knew, having lived this type of nightmare before, that the other two roaming guys, and whomever else was out there, will now have been alerted.

As my mind raced, as we ran, I knew I should have sent all three of those cock suckers to *never-never-land* on the permanent side of the photograph. I should have taken a *Kalashnikov.* Taken one, even though I hate guns.

There is no art to killing with a gun. None… But, my mind ran, as we ran.

We came up to this rather dense shrub filled area. It seemed an okay place to chill. I listened as Kyi Hlaing and I panted. I checked to see if I was still alive; if my heart had survived this dance with death. I was. It did. Her and I, we did not talk.

I heard yelling in the jungle. I knew people were pissed. And, I knew they were after us. *"Fuck me,"* I thought, *"Just out to make a little love in the bush, and I would have to run into this shit. Just my luck..."*

There's always an unlimited supply of assholes out there.

After a minute or three, we resumed the run.

By now, I was turned around and was not quite sure in which direction we were running. I began to listen for the voices of others at all times. All I knew was that I had to get away.

BANG! The shot of gunfire rang into the jungle. Then again. And again. I heard the bullets whistling by.

They were spraying the place, trying to weed us out.

BANG! Kyi Hlaing jerked and fell to the ground. *"Damn,"* I thought, *"Has she been hit?"*

I looked down to her, but it was just her ankle. Not much of a relief, however, for we had to make tracks and she held onto it as if it was seriously fucked up.

The gun spray continued to ring in through the foliage. I knew that it had virtually no chance of nailing us. But, it was not a good feeling.

The gun sounds became closer. The voices became closer. I told Kyi Hlaing that we had to move. With her hurt ankle, she said that she couldn't run.

My only alternative was to go solo. Go out and nail those *mutha fuckers.* Do what I should have done in the first place.

All fear was gone now. It was replaced by rage/by anger/by the need to protect my perfect love.

I had given them the opportunity once. The opportunity to live; to move on. They did not take/did not accept said opportunity. That would be their mistake/their downfall.

I hid her under some large leaves. I left her. I guess I should not have.

I moved through the jungle, like a leopard, like a cat on the prowl. They were many. I was few. But, I knew I had the edge. They were fools of the, *paid for hire breed.* They were *nothings* out there, attempting to get a necklace of ears to wear around their necks to prove that they were men.

I knew I was a man. I didn't have anything to prove.

I could hear their constant talk. *"Not much of warriors,"* I thought. Just scared little boys, needing to hear the voices of their friend to prove they were not alone.

"They're not over here. Do you see 'em there?"

Pussys...

I crawled, and through their talk, through their shots, I knew exactly where they were.

I heard one approach. I slid down under the green foliage that covered a tree, which lay to my left. He moved loudly, shooting periodically. Yelling to his *compatriots.*

BAM! I was up behind him. Snap, went his neck. This time I was not going to leave empty-handed. I grabbed his *Kalashnikov.* I grabbed a Ka-Bar style knife he had on his side.

I was on the move again...

Another guy talking,

"You hear me? Can you see me? Don't shoot this direction."

I came up behind his voice/his movements. I knew that it all had to happen fast or they would know that I was on the move; taking 'em down, one-by-one.

The atmosphere was right/ripe for victory. The only thing that I did not like is that they were moving in the direction of Kyi Hlaing. I had to work fast.

I approached number two. I had planned to stick this fucker with his friend's *stiv*. But, as I closed in, a twig snapped under my feet and he heard me. Fuck! He pivots, ready to shoot. I jumped in and rolled across the ground. I caught him midsection with my heel to his solar plexus. He was knocked down, stunned, but not out. He yelled, *"Help!"*

I jumped up. He jumped up. As he went for his pistol, I popped him with a stepping side kick to his throat. That, *mutha fucka,* was that. He was out, dead.

I grabbed his rifle and threw it into the dense vegetation.

Me, I moved back into the seclusion. I listened for the shots. But, heard none.

I knelt down for a moment: quiet, waiting. Then, I heard it; Kyi Hlaing's scream.

My heart felt ripped out. I ran through the jungle, like the fools those other guys were. Ran in the direction of her screams.

As I approached their location, I slowed down. I tried to hold myself back/tried to hold it together.

What were they doing to her? Her screams had stopped.

I moved in slow like a cobra. I could hear them laugh. My heart raced. My anger flared. I couldn't wait! There was no time!

I just walked right up to where they were. Walked right in; with gun in hand—locked and cocked.

They were standing there, in the verging dense jungle. Kyi Hlaing in front of them. All eyes on me.

"Well friend. I suggest you put down your weapon."
"Do it!"

Screamed the other guy inhabiting this situation.

I continued to look at them. Then with a yank, I could see Kyi Hlaing's head veer back. I was going to point and pull the *mutha fucking* trigger but I realized they had done the old guerilla number to her; they had tied the barrel of the gun to the neck of their intended victim. So, if I popped 'em, they popped her.

They were so stupid. They had probably seen that move in some old movie somewhere. Somewhere where the English had been translated into who knows what other language with subtitles.

But me, there was nothing I could do. I looked. I studied the situation. I dropped the gun.

This one then fuck-bucket walks up to me all smiles. I stare at him, eyeball to eyeball. He approaches and in a flash. *BAM!* He cold cocks me with the butt of his rifle. I fell to my knees.

"That was for my friends you killed."

I was dazed but not out. I was ready to go hand-to-hand to save Kyi Hlaing.

That is one of the first things that you've got to learn if you want to take it to the streets. Getting hit hurts. But, if your dazed, you can still fight. And, in fact, you can use that *dazed* to your advantage, because the next punch isn't going to hurt as much.

"Where's the rest of our men?"

Asks the guy, holding Kyi Hlaing.

"Dead, I suppose."

He turns to me,

"What are you, DEA?"

I didn't answer.

"Let's have this bitch, then kill him."

Now, I was really ready to party: kill or be killed. I knew if I got hit by one of those *Kalashnikov* bullets, I'd be *dead's-ville Daddy-O*. I'd been plugged by smaller calibers and it's no really big thing unless they hit you in just the right strategic place. But, a *Kalashnikov* bullet; well that *mutha fucka* would take me out fast. But, for her, Kyi Hlaing; yeah I'd leave this life. Leave it, if it would save her.

"No, we better move 'em back to camp. Tell the Colonel that things aren't going according to plan."

"Let's go..."

One of the two assholes grabbed up the rifle I had tossed on the ground, shoved me, shoved Kyi Hlaing, and we walked. They didn't try to tie me up or anything. I think they knew better—were worried about what that would lead to.

I saw that I had some advantage here. Didn't know how or why. Maybe it was my height—I towered over them. Maybe it was that I was white. Maybe it was that I had taken down a couple of their mates. I do not know. But, whatever it was, they possessed just a slight amount of fear about me. And, that can be a good *thAng,* when push comes to shove.

*　　*　　*

With a gun at my back, we walked for what seemed like several hours, up this trail into the depth of the wilds of Southeast Asia. I don't know, maybe be crossed into Thailand. Up there in the nowhere, boarders really don't mean too much.

As we walked, every moment my mind was filled with finding a way out, a way to save Kyi Hlaing. But, with her in that noose of a leash, I knew I could bail but that would leave her to the ways of these no good for nothing missionaries. The only thing that kept them from her, was me. They knew it. I knew it.

The trail led up through the red to brown soil colored rocks. The vegetation was yellow and green.

I continued to look at Kyi Hlaing as she limped up the trail. Her ankle was obviously fucked. But, they kept pushing her from behind with the barrel of the gun that was glued to the back of her neck.

I saw the tears run down her beautiful face. Was it I who had gotten her into this? Was it my desire for illusion, my propensity for chasing lust, or my love for her that had led to all of this? But, by whatever name/whatever form, it was my fault. I knew that. *"Why,"* was the only equitation, the only stipulation I could not find a reason for.

As I felt close to the pass-out point, (no water, smacked in the head, and all), we reached this small clearing in the trees. There were guards, dressed in dirty khaki clothing, carrying *Kalashnikovs,* waving us up, on, and in. We had entered the lion's den.

As we walked through the camp, there were several tents and maybe fifteen missionary commandos that I counted. They were talking. They were looking. They were pissed. They had already heard that I had wasted a couple of their *compadres.* They got up. They took to shoving me and taunting Kyi Hlaing.

But, worse still, as we walked through the camp, they had these bamboo cage type things; one held a man, the other held three local women that obviously had been used and abused. Fucking animals!

We walked up to this central tent *thAng.* They shoved me inside. Followed by several of the men and Kyi Hlaing still on her leash. This dude in his forties, sat at a table, drinking some tea or some shit like that.

The two men who brought us up saluted and said,

"We're sorry to inform you, Sir, the mission has not gone as planned."

The old man looked up.

"This DEA agent has killed..." A few names were mentioned.

The old man stood up. He walked up to me, very close, and looked me directly in the eyes. He spoke to me in broken English,

"You don't look like a DEA agent."

He gazed for a few more moments. A few moments that seemed to span an eternity. He then walked over to Kyi Hlaing. He looked her up and down. He pulled out a knife from a sheath that he wore on the side of his camouflage uniform. I jumped forward. Guns from all sides were pointed at me. He took the knife and cut the rope from Kyi Hlaing's neck. She fell to the floor. I could see the blood flowing from where the rope had cut into her neck. He then walks back to me.

"No, I don't think that you are a DEA man. I know all the DEA men sent to Burma. You're not one of them. What happened? Did my men bother your lady?"

He turned. He looked at his men. He continued.

"I don't know what it is with these men; they always want new ladies. Look at the ones they have outside..."

He walked around me. He returned to the front of me. He thinks for a moment.

"Though you are not a DEA man, you must be a trained killer to have killed so many of my men."

He walked up to me: face-to-face, eye-to-eye.

"Are you a trained killer?"

I say nothing. He studies me for a moment longer, then smiles,

"No matter. You can kill and that is all that is important. You see, we have a mission to do. We need to travel up river and move some opium for this man. You killed three of my men; you will do the job of three men. You will work with us."

"Three?" I questioned in my mind. *"I only numbered dos. But, then whose counting."*

Immediately, I emphatically stated,

"No, I won't!"
"Oh yes, you will!" He firmly replies.

He grabs Kyi Hlaing by the hair and pulls her up to standing position from where she crouched on the ground.

"You see, we have your lady. If she is enough that you have killed for her, then I imagine you will help us in order to get her back. Of course, my men will

147

have her while you are gone, but if you hurry, perhaps she will still be alive."

I studied his eyes. He was dead serious. I knew something had to be done/I knew, I had to do something.

Kyi Hlaing was just a toy to them, a pawn. She would just become a fuck-me toy; like those women out there in those bamboo cages. I could not let that happen. No, not to her.

My life, I didn't care about it. I should have died a long time ago. But, Kyi Hlaing, there was no way that I could let her endure a fate worse than death.

I looked around and noticed a 45-semi auto on his table. I had nothing to lose...

In a flash; I moved, I grabbed it, I cocked it.

In my mind, I felt I was already dead. So, when those are the odds that are dealt to you, what do you have to lose?

*   *   *

Have you ever done that in life; had something happen to you: a car accident, a fall, an experience, a whatever... And, like you feel this is it; you're dead? Well, I've had more than a few of those in my life. And, my nine lives are about up. Here/there again—I thought, *that was that.*

*   *   *

So, in that second of life; that second that seemed to last for an eternity, I pointed the gun right at him—right at his face. And though, all the guns in the tent were pointed at me, for some reason

148

they did not shoot. The men, if you can call them that, were confused as to what they should do.

I looked around, studied the situation; there was no way out. No, not for me. Certainly, no honorable way out for Kyi Hlaing.

I looked at her. I absorbed her image. Embraced—took in her living soul for that one last time. And, as if she knew; as if she agreed, she smiled at me.

I turned the gun on her and with one shot to the head, she was gone.

Blood and brains splattered. She fell to the ground.

Everyone looked at me; confused, in disbelief. I turned the gun to the colonel. I looked at him eye-to-eye. He smiled. I smiled. I said,

"A life for a life."

BAM! He was dead too.

Though I expected to be splatter right then/right there. I expected to immediately be placed in the realm of the ethereal, right next to Kyi Hlaing. But, all of the soldiers just looked at me.

I threw down the gun and walked out, shoving my way through the group of missionaries that had gathered around the hut. No one said a word.

I passed the cages where the women and the man were caged. I pulled a machete from out of a nearby tree and cut the ropes that tried them into their cells; cut them all loose. They ran.

Me, I continued forward. I walked down the mountain, numb; expecting that at any moment I would be popped in the back of the head by one of their bullets. No bullets came.

I guess the mercenaries, like puppies without their leash, didn't know what to do without a master. So, they did nothing.

I suppose it took a couple hours, but I found my way back to the river. I knew it was the place for there lay a bloated, being eaten by flies and ants, body of a gun for hire. I guess he was number three; the one I front kicked and his head snapped back. Guess I broke his neck. Whatever...

I sat down, up the river, away from him; not really knowing what to expect.

As time passed, a boat came. I didn't wave him over; he just pulled up. As he did, he noticed the missionary laying dead on the ground. He stared at the dead body a moment or three. Then, he looked at me. I said nothing.

I suppose he asked me where I was going; I don't really remember. But, I got in the boat and we moved down the river, picking a few people up, leaving a few off, as the day passed through its orange hues and turned into the night.

I got off the boat at this small dock. I assumed it was the end of the line. There waited a pickup truck of a transportation vehicle. I got in the back; said nothing to the driver, but he drove off.

I got back to town. Yes, my town, Kyi Hlaing's town; Keng Tung. It must have been way late. I walked through the empty streets, thinking of Kyi Hlaing's son—first his father and now the mother he would never have. No, not ever again.

Eventually, I found the way back to my guesthouse. I went in and lay on my bed, pulled the mosquito net over me. I don't know what I thought that night. Probably, why was I still alive? Why me, and not her; not my love, Kyi Hlaing.

Morning rose and I walked to the bus stop place. After about thirty, a bus pulls in. Didn't care where it was headed. Climbed onto the top side of the ride, laid down, and let the sun scorch my skin as we drove millions of miles across the countryside.

For better or for worse, the bus was headed for Mandalay.

Got to Mandalay. Got a plant to Rangoon.

In the Rangoon airport, I just walked up to the ticket counter, showed them my ticket, a week or so late; they said I could leave that afternoon. Told me, the plane from Bangkok was running late and there was one economy class seat left. Not my style, but what could I do?

Walked through customs, without a hitch. *"You're a little late,"* was the only comment I got post me tossing the dude a handful of my unusable *hundred*-kyat notes. The guy was happy to take 'em. I could tell, he knew how to get them exchanged.

I sat around for a few hours and waited for the plane to arrive. Watched as Aeroflot planes, from the U.S.S.R., continued to fly in. Figured another take-over, coup, or something was in the works. But, who cared.

I sat there in the pouncing, pouring heat. I sat there alive, while Kyi Hlaing was dead. I sat there, trying to reaffirm/trying to tell myself/prove to myself that nothing was permanent. That everything only lasts for the shortest moment in time. I tried to tell myself it was all just destiny. A destiny that I did not/could not ever understand. I try to tell myself... But, all I felt was, what had I done? Why did I dance into the arms of danger again, only to, (again), take an innocent bystander down with me? And wonder why—why does life always have to end?

The plane came. I few back to Bangkok.

Conclusion

I once had this girlfriend; she often would tell me that I was always fighting, that I made everything a battle.

Life is *Jehad.* Life is a holy war. It takes no prisoners and there is no escape.

I do not live life; I attack life.

If you live life, like all the poets, all the pacifists, it controls you; you are powerless. Attack life and you own it.

www.ingramcontent.com/pod-product-compliance
Lightning Source LLC
Chambersburg PA
CBHW050659290626
47170CB00015B/2089